SWEET DECEIT

K A DUGGAN

Sweet Deceit
This edition published in 2019
Copyright © K A Duggan

The moral right of the author has been asserted.
ISBN 9781706924227

Printed and bound by CreateSpace
DBA of On-Demand Publishing, LLC
www.createspace.com

Chapter 1

Felicity

Current mood – Philosophical with a chance of bad decision making.
Regret level – 50/50

My decision was made in the blink of an eye. Which, for someone as decisively challenged as I am is not only out of character but should be deeply worrying. I guess once you've reached your limit nothing else matters. Circumstances made it so and I never looked back.

All it took was my last visit and the answer to my problems became crystal clear.

Escape.

It was the only logical thought my brain managed to desperately grasp on to.

Just go. Run.

And as I stepped out into the car park, the rain falling all around me, inadvertently masking my tears, I decided to listen for once. It's amazing how and when clarity chooses to present itself and what that moment of clarity can do for your soul. I made a vow to myself, only honouring it wasn't going to be as straightforward as the thought of it alluded to be.

Considering recent developments, it shouldn't be my main concern. But it is. Because I've let it be. I've allowed it to push everything else aside. The other issues are inconsequential because I have this. It came along and announced its importance like a radio in my head that won't switch off. It's deafeningly loud, drowning out every other concern and ensuring it's the only thought I can focus on, because the other questions... they're even more ludicrous. It's a thought that I hoped could remain behind an elusive fog.

But at some point, fog always clears, revealing the way forward once again.

The idea had been present for weeks, lingering somewhere in the recesses of my mind. Gradually it began gnawing at me from the inside out. Begging me to fulfil its wishes. I'd managed to exile it, for the most part, hidden in the background, concealed by shadows. I stubbornly ignored its taunts and tricks like a petulant child as it screamed at me to acknowledge it. I'd done well, but on this particular day, it upped the ante, as though it could sense my fragility. I didn't want to think about what I'd just left, what I was going home to or what my future held so I allowed it in. Little by little. I let this consume me instead. It seemed the lesser of two evils.

I judged myself as was only right to do so, I let myself burn with shame for even thinking it but only for a fraction of a second.

Only, now it's free due to sheer persistence and I guess as much as I don't want to, I have to decipher the answer.

What could make a sensible woman journey halfway across the world on nothing more than a whim?

It's not a trick question. But there are multiple answers.

The main answer's easy, right? At least, it should be.

Clearly a boy. No, scratch that – a man.

A man that has absolutely no idea I'm coming. A man that likely has no desire to see me. A man I can't stop thinking about. No, obsessing about would be closer to the truth. Yet, I'm going anyway.

Maybe it's as simple as... I'm not a sensible woman. I *used to be*. Being sensible is how I was raised, it's all I know. My safeguard. Irresponsibility isn't in my genes as far as I know. But then genes have proven to be fickle. Only passing down certain traits as it sees fit. You can't pick and choose what you 'get' and you only get what you're given. Inheritance is funny like that. But to be acting on this leads me to believe maybe the real me is less suppressed than I've always believed.

Reckless. Free-spirited. All words one wouldn't possibly associate with me... before.

I have the answer.

The real answer.

I just don't want to acknowledge it. I never wanted to give life to it so I kept locking it away, pushing it aside with all the other swirling thoughts. Pretending that dismissing it would lead to its disappearance once and for all and I could concentrate on forging ahead with my crazy plans.

This spur of the moment decision has run away with me and is now completely out of hand. I know this because I'm not completely crazy. But still, *I have* to do it. This infatuation I've nurtured has become too huge to ignore. It's an itch I absolutely have to scratch and sanity doesn't stand a chance. I know what will happen when I get there. *I know.* Yet I'm still packing as though I'm off to my happily ever after. Because they must be real, right? Why else would we be brought up on such stories of hope for the future if there is no truth to them?

This has played out in my dreams repeatedly and it nearly always ends the same way. He'll likely open the door, maybe if I'm lucky, recognise me on a sub-conscious level and then slam it in my face as he launches 'fuck off!' at me.

I'll then probably end up with a restraining order.

Go big or go home. Right?

In my case, I should probably just stay home. Actually, there's no probably about it; I *really* should stay home. I've been left with huge responsibilities that at the moment I have no inclination to face. Some would call this running away, fleeing from something too painful to stand and conquer. Some would say I'm a coward. Shirking my responsibilities. But the opinions of others have never concerned me.

Being flighty has never been attractive to me. I was raised better than this, but now, everything is in question. The weight of what faces me has left me with no choice. I'm desperate to escape and evade just for a momentary reprieve. A lapse in time where I don't have to make the right choices, where I can be someone else. Someone that doesn't have it all together. Someone like all the other someone's tripping through life, having the ability to learn from their mistakes instead of always making the correct choice first time.

So, I keep telling myself, I'm not running away from my newfound burdens ... I'm grasping my chance at living. At least, that's how I dress it up to myself. That kind of thought process is definitely preferable, it's prettier and more acceptable. And this is why I'm really going... there's a tiny chance he'll let me in. Not just to his home but in time maybe into his heart. Granted it's more like miniscule but still a chance nonetheless. A tiny possibility that's grown wings and is taking me along for the flight of my life. The romance books I read have filled my head with notions. Notions that real life, if we want it badly enough, can play out like a work of fiction.

See, I don't have anyone to rein me in. No parents, no friends. No well-meaning colleagues or neighbours.

Except for Gerry, I suppose. But for the time being, I'm not taking his calls.

I'm isolated. At least, that's how it feels. How I've always felt.

Alone. With no one that can relate to these feelings.

For the first time in my life, I'm completely and solely reliant on myself.

I've never minded my own company, in fact, I enjoyed it. I was encouraged to be a loner. Mingling was strictly prohibited. I was stalled at every avenue of normality from childhood. The experiences other children took for granted, I longed for. Homeschoolingwas the main barricade between myself and my peers. My parents had so many expectations for me that also living up to society's equally high standards would have been impossible. So, I have no one to warn me how crazy, idiotic and downright stupid I'm being. The rational side of me tries. It really does, but the hopeful side always overrules.

My life has been a series of secluded, sheltered memories. And I'm desperate to make new ones... better ones.

Real ones.

Because now, I loathe my own company. The silence. Such deafening silence.

I didn't know the quiet could be so loud.

I didn't know solitude could be so overbearing.

I didn't know 'in sickness and in health', applied without the marriage.

And it's not just the conversation I miss, simple things like a smile or laugh, a reassuring hug... anything from anyone.

Just so I know I'm still alive.

So I know I still matter.

So I know I still count in this big bad world.

So I know I still am *someone's* whole world.

Because without something as basic as human interaction I'll wither faster than if I went without sustenance. It's a basic need in life. The simplest. But only when it's taken away do we realise how truly important and essential it is. When we're left with this unexplainable void. I want to live the life I yearn for not the life I've repeatedly been told I should lead. I want more. I crave more. So much more than what's been expected of me.

I want to live life to its fullest because we never know what it has in store for us. We can't predict what's around the corner. We only have today and today I've chosen.

Freedom.

And, for the first time in my life, I have it. What I do with it is all open to interpretation.

What I want to do with it I probably shouldn't. But who's going to hold me back?

For the first time in my life, I can be *me*.

The real me, whoever she is.

Discovering her is what life is all about.

———

I admit this strategy of mine could be planned better, *should be* planned more thoroughly, paying attention to detail like I was raised to but that isn't what spontaneity is about. And I've decided being responsible isn't all it's cracked up to be. This man is no ordinary man, he isn't someone you can just strike a conversation up with. He doesn't do pointless, polite chit chat. You can only get on his radar by appealing to his interests, by having more depth to your discussions. A little stroking of his ego also goes a long way. He doesn't beat around the bush, he doesn't fake niceties. He's the most real person I've encountered on social media.

Shit! Did I leave that part out?

I know what you're thinking. I also thought about the wackos that meet on dating websites.

This is different.

I'm not entirely sure how... but it is. For one – I didn't find him on a dating website. Nope. Forget Tinder and Plenty of Fish. I found my love match on regular old Facebook... He just doesn't know it. Because for now, it's totally one-sided. But I have plans and making this a two-way street is my main objective.

I'm a fan of his and no he isn't a celebrity – I'd never stalk one of those. We're friends... as much as we can be only communicating online. I pray daily that I'm not being *catfished* because his personality is amazing but let's be honest, the pictures I've seen of him were the first draw. You have to be attracted to someone first and foremost, the great personality is a bonus. If I get there and he doesn't really exist, if Ash turns out to be Bob or Fred or some other random dude I'll be shattered.

I can't totally explain his pull. What caught me in his web initially were his words, his mind, the beautifully crafted story he had created. A quick internet search then revealed he was hot, insanely, unfairly so. I've never seen a person sculpted to such perfection and I couldn't stop my fingers from flying over the keyboard and sending him a message.

That would have been it.

But he responded.

Ever since then if he replies to my comments or messages even with the slightest remark, my body goes crazy. Do you remember your first love? Or your first lust? The guy that caused you to walk a fine line between obsession and rationale. The guy that could walk into a room and your belly would flip, your heart would thump and your legs would shake. If they rang you, you lit up from inside and butterflies ran amok. Everything about them just did it for you.

Yeah, well that's what he does. So as much as I should ignore it, I'm not. We only get one life. I'm going to grab mine, hold on so tight and agree with everything it suggests.

He's been the best and most welcoming distraction for the last six months. Ever since I stumbled across him accidentally. Not that I truly believe it was accidental – fate has a purpose, it can only point us the right way, show us a path and if we're lucky enough give us a nudge in the right direction. Our paths aligned because of a series of shitty events. I have to believe this option only became available to me to change my future for the better. More than anything I wholeheartedly believe that if we can just meet, even for the briefest of moments our eternity will be cemented.

He has no idea I'm crushing on him. He's never seen a picture of me and he doesn't know my real name, so I guess if anyone is the catfish here it's me. I immersed myself in his life from afar. He's briefly touched on the females who throw themselves at him, who act like idiots in his presence and this is why I can't let him know I'm coming. I don't want to be judged like them. I want to see if he really is as good in person as he is behind a computer screen. I need to witness face to face if the supposed truths he's told hold up, or if I've been wrapped up in more lies, if he's also sold me falsity. I need him to be my escape because like I said before... I have no-one else.

I'm not going to be held back by fears. Because what I do now, rightly or wrongly, will be what I look back on when I'm old and frail and stuck in some nursing home and you know what? I'll be able to smile at the insane antics I got up to. The impossible situations I got through because I had guts. I chose to really live, come what may.

Even if right now it makes me cry.

I will be able to smile.

We should all take more chances. Instead of building up the worst that can happen scenarios, we should just do it. Half the people we concern ourselves with over what their opinion will be and how we'll be viewed – don't matter. These people are jealous that they can't break free. That they can't set out their own destiny instead of being held back by what's expected. They're chained. Shackled. And if they can't break free they expect others to share in their misery.

Being good is exhausting. This, though alien feels liberating.

Who wants mediocre?

Who wants to be part of the norm?

So, I'm opting to be part of the abnormal. The dreamers, the wanderers, those that don't fit so compactly into society. And that's okay. My dreams might come true by taking this risk and if they don't...

I'll move on to the next pipe dream.

Felicity

Current mood – Slightly Extroverted bordering on impulsive
Regret level - Undecided

The most ridiculous part of this whole plan is that I've never travelled before, never ventured further than my hometown of London. Fear held me back, something my parents fiercely instilled in me and though I've decided to ignore it, to push through and banish those intrusive thoughts, sometimes they fight back harder and break through. My parents were a weird breed, completely successful, confident and go-getting but, they kept me on a tight leash. That leash became even tighter once my father left, my mother's overprotectiveness unleashing full force. We were practically recluses.

Technically, my travel plans aren't across the world, but to me they may as well be. *I have a huge tendency for exaggeration.* I've never flown, so even a one hour journey seems lengthy to a newbie. I looked into other ways of getting to him, but car and Ferry would have taken too long. I don't have that kind of patience, so I sucked up my gnawing fears and booked a flight; my destination, Ireland.

In my current no shits given mood I make it to the airport. I make it past all the check-ins and the queues and get on the plane. Ticking each new experience off my invisible checklist whilst inwardly patting myself on the back for my bravery. I spend my time aboard the plane clutching the armrest for dear life convinced we'll crash and that I'll die. Flying is not fun, not the tiniest bit enjoyable at all. And I *try* to enjoy it, I really do. It's a new experience so I aim to soak it up but I guess shirking the ingrained lessons I've been taught all my life are harder to shake than I wanted them to be. White knuckle rides are a thrill I won't be seeking again.

New - I want.

Terrifying - I don't.

But then, aren't all new things terrifying? Taking that leap of faith into the unknown and hoping you come out the other end unscathed?

I chalk it up as a means to an end and the relief that it's over is immense. I make a quick stop off at my hotel to drop off my suitcase and then flag a taxi down to make a beeline straight for his.

My ride is spent with no trepidation whatsoever. No nerves, doubts or second thoughts. Just eagerness, anticipation and excitement. Urgency bubbling in my veins. How I don't bounce around in my seat like a bottle of pop I don't know.

I get to my destination in record time realising in my haste that I didn't stop to freshen up or change. My unrealistic expectations propelled me forward and I find myself walking through the front door to his apartment building. This entire trip, from the plane journey to this exact moment I've had a one-track mind - get to him. It's been my only focus, playing in my head on a loop. I haven't allowed myself time to stop and think because that's when the insanity will smack me in the face and push me off course. *I just have to get to him and away from where I came.*

Then I'm in a brightly lit, freshly painted hallway standing right outside his door. How I attained his address is unimportant but let's just say I'd be seriously up a shit creek for how I came about that information.

And now reality decides to come knocking.

This is nuts.

Thinking I'm seizing the day and all that sounds exhilarating. Brave and fearless. I talk a good talk. *Even if it is to myself.* But this is just... there are no words for this.

I chose my outfit carefully before boarding the plane, taking hours agonising over achieving the right look, going for what I hope is some kind of understated sexy but with a professional twist. I have no idea what passes for fashionable. Comfort has always been my main aim, and onesies fit that bill. So I feel ridiculous. And probably look it too. Especially now my carefully ironed clothes are no longer pristine, creases are present in every item all thanks to the flight. My long blonde hair no longer straightened to within an inch of its life but determinedly gaining volume. I always wondered why those girls I used to look at in the street, or in shops always looked so 'put together'. I couldn't understand why they'd spend so much of their time wasting it on primping and preening. I've never had to consider my appearance and the effect it could have on others, but now? I mean, what does one wear to meet the guy they've fixated on? I doubt sweats would cut it somehow.

My parents were huge advocates for *'it's what's inside that counts'* and *'brains over beauty'* which thinking about it now might mean they thought I was ugly and that's why they pushed so hard for me to be an intelligent frump. I wrinkle my nose at the thought. Do mirrors lie? I thought parents didn't so it just goes to show how intelligent I really am. What if he's repulsed by me?

I shake my head to clear those wandering thoughts or I'll be stuck contemplating them all day. And now I'm standing here, mere feet away from my crush and only friend in the entire world, worried about the effect I'll have on him. But I can't muster the courage to knock. What would I say - 'hi' and then what? What am I really expecting to happen? In fantasies, guys say they'd love a woman to turn up on their doorstep and offer all sorts of obscene things to them. They reckon they'd drag them inside, have a few hours of fun and it can be checked off their bucket list. But really, what guy would ask no questions? What guy would let a borderline stalker/stranger into their home?

Definitely not this guy. He values privacy and explaining how I tracked him down could get me in a whole heap of trouble. *Okay. Enough stalling. Knock on the door. You've come this far. Whatever happens, happens.*

I take a load of deep breaths, fiddle with my outfit needlessly, because other than taking it all off, I can't change it, though my pencil skirt now feels like a mini skirt, my khaki blouse has too many buttons open, or does it? *Shit, I don't know.*

I knock. Then fidget. Then wait.

My palms are sweating and slippery, in fact, as a drop of cold sweat makes its way down my back I realise my whole body is. If attractive is what I was going for, I've achieved the complete opposite.

The door flies open almost in impatience and the first hint of sensibleness slaps me in my face.

This is a stranger.

He could be a psychopath. A murderer. A sexual predator.

The list is neverending. Panic sets in. Wrapping around my throat as my nervous, cold sweat turns to icy fingers mocking me and my idiocy. I'd never be found, no one knows I'm here. It'd be easy to make me disappear because no one would come looking. I doubt anyone would even notice.

He clears his throat not too subtly and I risk peeking at him if for nothing else than to have a description if he is a creep and I manage to escape. My heart clenches. I'm suddenly very aware of how off the charts this is. My mouth won't work as my tongue deserts me. Which is good because I have no speech planned, no explanation for my showing up here unannounced. I never thought that far ahead.

I stand and stare at him, drinking him in. *Oh my God*, he's real and in the flesh. So much better in the flesh. So much better than the images I've repeatedly dreamt of. I should've been worried about the effect *he'd* have on *me*. My already dodgy breathing goes to shit as he stands before me. I feel light-headed like I'm seconds away from my face meeting the floor. My heart continues to pound against my rib cage. My fingers twitch from the insane need to reach out and touch him, not only to check he's real but to use him as an anchor to banish my dizziness, but I can't act like a total freak. Let's be honest – I'm being freaky enough as is. I almost squeal in relief that he's who he's meant to be. He's not an imposter, there's no Bob or Fred trickery here.

He frowns at me, as though I'm an inconvenience, giving me a quick once over and says, "You just going to stand there or are you coming in?"

Sexy accent that I can't quite place. The Irish lilt to his words almost making me falter. I'm concentrating so hard on watching his lips moving that I almost don't hear the words he speaks. *That voice.* Super sexy, rich and much deeper than I imagined. How I'm still standing I don't know, but then my brain registers something. *Okay, that was easy.* Way too easy. I expected some fierce words, maybe grovelling on my end. Begging. Some explaining. *Hell*, lots of explaining. Not an open invite.

I nod and walk into his apartment with a faked assuredness as though my legs are perfectly steady instead of the elastic bands they really feel like. It smells of bleach or some type of cleaning agent, it hangs in the air burning my nostrils as if he's had a mad cleaning spree. *Almost as though he was expecting me.*

He brushes past me and as he does I take in his dark jeans, black T-shirt and mostly just his backside. His scent wafts past me, clean linen. "I'm sorry but I've managed to double book myself, this will have to be a quick tour." He says as he walks ahead of me.

A quick tour? What have I walked into? Who does he think I am?

Before I have a chance to ponder further or correct him he sweeps his arm out "Living room" he says and I bite down the urge to reply with a sarcastic comment. He walks off as though expecting me to continue following and I do, still focusing on staring at him, he opens another door to the right "Bathroom" he says and now I'm really baffled. Why is he telling me what each room is? Why hasn't he questioned my appearing on his doorstep out of the blue? What is with this crazy tour? I bite down a nervous giggle at the absurdity.

"This is the spare room." He continues in an overly bored tone, opening another door and turning to face me. He's beautiful. I'd never tell him that because he's a man and that's not a manly enough compliment, but he is. Jet black hair, brown eyes, and the longest eyelashes. I almost sigh in the style of a Disney princess. My hand flies to my mouth, covering the snort I almost released.

"So, what do you think?" he asks, turning and facing me before quickly glancing at his watch.

I press pause on my inner dialogue making me realise he's not asking about my thoughts on *him*, my only reason for being here. I reluctantly let him pull me back to the present.

"Umm, uh... your home is lovely." I stutter. Really, I wouldn't know, I haven't paid any attention to the rooms. I'm still in shock that I'm in. That he's talking to me and... looking at me. We're *finally* face to face and all I can do is stare. There's something on the tip of my tongue but I can't figure out if it's something totally inappropriate like *I love you* or something as equally dodgy like *It's me, your friend from your computer.* Either way, I bite my cheek to stop from blurting anything.

His brows rise "Not from around here?"

"What gave me away?"

"The accent for one. Look, I'm late for something so do you want the room or not?" his tone oozes cool detachment.

"Huh?"

"You're here for the spare room, right?" he questions as his brow raises.

"Yeah, right." I agree quickly.

"So? Are you my new roommate or not?" It may be wishful thinking but I'm sure I hear a hint of desperation in his voice, like he needs me to accept. *It probably is my wishful thinking.*

"Me?" I blurt.

He squints at me and I mentally collect myself. *Don't do it* my inner angel warns but my inner devil practically jumps up and down compelling me to answer "Yes, I'll take it." My inner angel shakes her head, rolls her eyes and states *You're going to hell.*

But Ash smiles as if I've just solved all his problems and that's the guilt trip I need. *What am I doing?*

"Good. So, uh if you have the first month's rent, we're good to go." He waffles on 'reminding' me of the price and running through some ground rules. He takes me over to a kitchen island and shows me the paperwork.

"Right, so the paperwork is here, and this is the spare key. I've signed already so feel free to peruse it and if happy it's a done deal. I know this is unorthodox and I'm really sorry to dump you like this, but I really do have to go. I'll be back later so feel free to make yourself at home, acclimatise, whatever and if you need to move your things in while I'm gone, please do. We can catch up later, roomie?" As he talks, I pretend to read the contract in front of me but not one word registers. I know that I hand over a wad of cash because unlike most people in this day and age contactless payments aren't for me and I would lose a bank card much easier than a sum of cash. I'm still not paying complete attention, just watching his lips move. Reacting on autopilot, which is always what you want when completing such a transaction.

"Okay." I agree as if in the space of 10 minutes I didn't just commit a terrible crime of passion.

And just like that my crush is gone, leaving me to stare around my new home. Wondering what the hell just happened and what have I got myself into. That was weird. Too easy. I'm relieved on the one hand but who does that? *Who does this?* He didn't even get my name, didn't vet me. Run through expectations or caveats. He simply agreed I could move in and handed over a key. But then who am I to question someone else's sanity? Mine is clearly overdue a check-up.

I'm completely lost now. I hug myself to rid the extreme bout of vulnerability before spinning in a circle, looking around the space. It's a decent size for an apartment, clean and open plan with only a half wall as a divider between the lounge and kitchen allowing for great sightlines from either room. The lounge comprises of a huge black leather corner settee, coffee table, and bookshelf. No photos, nicknacks or plant life grace this room. Nothing to indicate his character apart from his reading collection.

I guess I should get my case from the hotel and check out? Then come back and plan my next move better. *Meticulously.* From what I thought I knew of him he's guarded but to leave a complete stranger alone in his home shows he's actually too trusting which could be a huge advantage for me. Or he simply may have a screw loose, I could steal anything, trash the place or plant recording equipment for all he knows, and he left me to it. *Stupid move Ash.* I start faffing around indecisively, plumping the cushions and straightening books to calm my mind. Anything to quell the nervous energy coursing through my veins. Knocking jolts me mid tidy and I jump as though I've been caught doing something I shouldn't. I creep towards the door and peep through the spy hole.

Standing on the other side is a woman. A very beautiful woman and I mentally kick myself. Shit! This must be the girlfriend. Because why wouldn't a hot guy like him have someone. He's never mentioned a girlfriend when we chat but maybe she's an out of bounds topic. She knocks again while I'm frozen in place with dismay and a fit of odd jealousy I have no right to own.

In a moment of bravery, I throw caution to the wind and open the door wide. We size each other up in that bitchy way women do, as though we're competition to one another. She's perfectly poised, long blonde hair and inquisitive brown eyes. She cranes her neck looking past me to the living room, searching as though she's familiar with the place. I raise my brows at her as she refocuses her attention on looking me up and down "Can I help you?"

"I was expecting Ash. I'm here about the room." She looks past me as she speaks, angling her neck again as if I'm hiding her prey and hoping to catch a sight of him.

Crap. The room I just stole from underneath her. How the hell do I explain this? At the same time, I'm hugely relieved she isn't any competition. Then again just because she isn't his girlfriend, doesn't mean he doesn't have one.

"The room," I repeat like a moron. She snaps her gaze at me, her nose wrinkling like I am one and I stumble over my words "Um... I'm sorry ... but it's already been taken."

She narrows her eyes as she runs them over me again "By you?" and the disdain in her voice is hard to miss. It gets my back up. This is supposed to be my fresh start, the revealing of the new me and the new me won't be spoken to like trash, so I lean against the door, pin her with what I hope is an intimidating glare and reply "Yes by me. Do you have a problem with that?" *Come on, challenge me.* I feel very territorial both over the man that lives here and the house itself. I didn't fly all this way to fail and I won't be run off by a botox bitch.

She smirks "He's such an arsehole. I trekked all the way over here for nothing."

"I'll be sure to let him know." I smile sweetly

"Was worth a try." She says but I feel like it was more to herself than for my benefit.

She turns on her heel and I swear I hear her mutter under her breath but I don't quite catch whatever bitchy remark it was.

I close the door and throw myself on his corner couch. That was my first time standing up to someone, fighting over something that isn't rightfully mine. I didn't cower, give in or back away like I used to. I feel proud of myself even though I have no right to. I am the one in the wrong but this smug feeling is something I definitely like.

This new me is someone I'm definitely on board with.

Chapter 3

Felicity

Current mood – Dreamy
Regret level– Ask me in the morning.

I decided to listen to some sense and left the apartment to return to my hotel room. I left Ash a note explaining that I'll be moving in tomorrow. I needed some space from his... space and smell, time to digest what I've actually done. Tearing myself away when I had ample opportunity to snoop through his things was a good call. The right call. But I feel like I missed out. I've duped the poor guy and when he finds out, which he inevitably will, well, the shit's going to hit the fan. Our first meeting didn't go down the way I planned. Hell, it wasn't even close to what I thought might happen.

Right now, I wish I had a friend to phone. I know I'm in need of 'the talk' but I'm taking it as a sign from the universe that this was meant to be. Why else would it have been so easy? Clearly, a higher power pointed me on this path and just keeps guiding me.

I climb in to bed, wanting to be fresh-faced for my next encounter with him. Maybe, tomorrow he'll spend the day with me? We'll bond, find what we have in common, connect. All manner of wishful thinking runs through my mind until I've convinced myself tomorrow he'll fall head over heels in love with me. I laugh at myself and those whimsical thoughts. I pull out my notepad knowing that this definitely makes a journal entry – the first time I met Ash needs to be documented for a rainy day read.

Journal entry

I did it. I met Ash. I actually got my arse on a plane and flew to meet the guy of my dreams. And he was real, not some overweight, middle-aged fake. I've always thought of Ash as sexy but thought he'd photoshopped his profile pic or stolen some model's identity for the purposes of meeting women online. In person though, sexy doesn't quite sum up how insanely, unfairly panty melting this guy is. Not only did I meet him, but I've ended up living with him. I'm not quite sure how as it happened too quickly to understand. This was never the plan but I'm going to run with it, see where it leads. Fate is my friend. She'd never steer me wrong, right?

Once finished I lie down marvelling at the smile on my face. I never thought smiling would be on the cards so soon, if ever again. Taking chances works – who knew? Now I'm over the first hurdle, I need to plan. I never thought I'd get through the door so the fact that I'm now going to be living with him is a blessing and a problem. He's bound to ask questions about my life, my job and so many other things I don't have answers to. I hate lying, it's a new concept for me but I guess, for now, I have to. Truth isn't always the best policy contrary to popular belief. I need to tread carefully and play this by ear.

I drift off and like I do most nights I dream of him – laughing with me, looking at me as though I'm his whole world, holding hands, kissing, just being together. Fantasizing.

The following evening, I find myself the other side of his door, just as nervous as the day before. Yet again it's taken me nearly a whole day to decide what to wear and in the end, I settled on boring old skinny jeans and a v-neck top. I really can't break out my favourite day wear yet so I've dressed like normal people for the last few days. Ease the guy in gently. I tied myself up in knots about coming back, yet here I am continuing with my trail of lies. I could have put an end to this before it even really began but coulda, shoulda, woulda's no longer belong in my repertoire.

I lift a shaking hand, repulsed when I see the state of my now bitten down nails and knock.

Silence.

I wait a beat and knock again, my heart pounding.

The door opens and my mouth decides to bless me with an overabundance of saliva, convincing me that it's escaping from the side of my mouth. He's stood before me in nothing but black boxers, his hair dishevelled from sleep, mussed nicely and I audibly gulp. *Good lord!* He looks me up and down as though he's trying to place me. The minute he does, the moment he actually *sees* me his face changes from mild curiosity to annoyance.

"You have a key." He tells me flatly

I fidget under his scrutiny "I didn't want to just let myself in. I thought you might have changed your mind."

His eyebrows shoot up "And you think I'd just keep your money?"

This isn't going well. At least I got through the door yesterday. And his body on show isn't helping me to think clearly. My eyes flick to his torso again and linger. What I'd give to touch it. I have a mini daydream about doing just that, my hand sliding over the firm ridges, before I'm snapped back to reality. *Shit*, I think my ovaries just had an attack of some kind, something similar to a heart attack, just a completely different part of the body. I know this because of the way they're spasming and if they didn't suffer some long term damage then some other internal organ is in dire need of medical attention. I press my legs together, the over-whelming urge to clench takes over and I feel myself blush as my body fails me in ways I not only never expected but have never experienced.

He clears his throat and when I snap my head up and look at him his eyes are twinkling with amusement. Damn. I wonder if he recognises the ovary distress look, it must happen regularly around him.

"I forgot the question." I admit meekly and my blush deepens at being caught ogling.

"Something else capture your attention?"

Oh God. Ground open up and swallow me, please?

"No!" I protest too loudly as I shake my head "I just... I have a short attention span." I wince at my answer. *Now, he's going to think I'm an idiot. I am an idiot.* I mentally face palm. What the hell kind of confession was that? What a perfect time to be afflicted with mouth diarrhoea. He's turned me from a former specimen of female togetherness into a drooling mess. If only he knew what his superpower is. *Maybe he does.*

"You're easily distracted... hmm." And he grins. At me. I've never swooned before so can't be sure but I think I swoon on the spot.

I start fidgeting, my face is burning. And all I can think about is getting away from him. "Maybe I should come back another time?" I try but the breathy tone in my voice lets me down.

He grins as he takes this in "But, you're here now."

"You um, you obviously weren't expecting me and aren't ready for me."

He leans against the doorframe, unashamedly, crossing his arms casually as he does so, as though he has all the time in the world to have this conversation regardless of the fact that he's practically naked "I'm always ready."

I swallow. Why does everything out of his mouth sound like an innuendo? Or is that just my dirty mind breaking free from the jail I cage it in? His words are perfectly chosen just to trip me up. I'm dying on the spot. Trying to talk and act naturally without touching him which is the hardest thing I've ever had to focus on. Harder than studying for exams. Harder than finding out truths have been lies. Harder than having him in my life from afar. And all those thoughts about *hard* has me moving my gaze from those glorious abs and down to his boxers.

He steps back a fraction indicating that I can come in but he purposely leaves only enough room so I have to brush past his body as I shimmy through. I enter with my back to his front and the second our bodies touch I have to close my eyes as I freeze in place. Then I'm moving quickly, dragging my suitcase on wheels along with me as if he's going to bite and I put much needed distance between us.

"I'll be fine if you want to go get dressed." I breathe out. *Please get dressed.*

"I am dressed." He teases as he closes the door and I gulp.

"Is this how you normally walk around your home?"

"Absolutely. I'm at home, it's comfortable. Feel free to adopt the same clothing style... in the name of comfort, of course."

"Of course." I mumble and for the briefest of seconds, I question why him walking around barely clothed is a problem for me. *Maybe I am insane.*

"Does my body offend you? Because if so, I could be persuaded to cover up the hideousness."

"What? No. It's not that... it's uh... um"

"You trip over your words a lot. It's cute."

My eyes narrow at his condescending comment *Oh, no Ash I'm far from cute.* I level my gaze at him "You're very distracting and you know it. Teasing me is mean, and flaunting..." I wave my hand in the direction of him "... that is just, well you must know the effect ... so I guess... that's it." I feel like I've just run a marathon. The strong stance I was trying to take over his cute comment failed miserably.

"I don't know. You'll have to help me understand. What effect do I have?" he leans against the counter casually crossing one ankle over the other.

"Please stop." I whisper averting my eyes to the floor. I think I'm going to combust on the spot. I know he's just playing with me but I can't take it. I grip the handle of my suitcase like it's a lifeline, a barrier to the heat he elicits.

Silence ensues. An awkward silence, in which time I contemplate walking out and giving up on this pipe dream. I've had daydreams about flirting between us, but the reality is so intense I need time to catch up to my runaway heart. I've never been a flirt. I don't quite know the tricks that other girls do. I always kept to myself, kept my head down and studied like my life depended on it. I'm way out of my depth.

I hear him shuffling around but I stay in my spot. Staring at the floor, the only safe place to stare.

"Coffee?"

I look up and he's wearing a grey t-shirt, the boxers are still on show but he's at least made an attempt to cover up more, to try and make me feel comfortable and my breathing starts to regulate.

I nod and join him in his kitchen, taking a seat at his breakfast bar. Watching him move around collecting cups.

"One sugar please." I tell him

"You know how I like mine." A voice behind me says and once again I freeze. We're not alone and the voice belongs to a female. Tears start to build and the will power it takes to contain them is painful. I flick my eyes up to Ash and he chews his bottom lip, his gaze roams over me and then over to the mystery woman behind me.

I stand up quickly making the legs of the seat scrape harshly on the floor "I think I'll go and unpack instead." I meet his intense gaze and hope he can see the begging in mine to just agree and not make me feel any more awkward.

"Okay."

I release a huge breath, one of relief and despair and snatch up the handle of my suitcase, taking my frustration out on it, I yank expecting the wheels to glide along with my quick march, only it has other ideas as it catches against the breakfast bar chair leg, pulling me back and causing me to land on my arse. Silence follows, hearing a pin drop would be a piece of piss. I keep my back to them both, the tears that were building before now threatening to spill over. I spring off the floor and as Ash starts to ask if I'm okay I nod without glancing back and continue wandering to my room as quickly as I can, avoiding any eye contact with the woman.

Once in my room, I discard my case and slump against the closed door. My , tears burn the back of my eyelids but I refuse to let them fall. I'm beyond embarrassed. And not only because of my unladylike fall. *I'm so stupid.* I stay slouched in this position until my already sore bum goes numb and that's the only reason I listen to my body's command to move. Eventually, when I'm feeling slightly more composed, I press my ear against it to listen to them but all I can hear is muffled voices. *Probably laughing at me.* Which is just another reality check I needed. He had sex last night. Maybe all day long for all I know. And, why wouldn't he? Just because I've built up a relationship between us in my head doesn't mean it's fact. It's a delusion. I can finally see that and it's a sobering thought. Explains why he was so perky and chipper this evening as opposed to his closed-off self I had the pleasure of meeting yesterday. He got laid.

What the hell do I do now? I debate unpacking my clothes but know I likely won't be staying after today. I feel like I've been cheated on, only I can't kick off, can't yell at him and demand to know why he'd hurt me this way. I have to keep pulling myself up and away from my imaginary life with him to the very real image hitting me in the face. I pull out my laptop instead and lay down on the bed with it resting on my propped legs. I browse Facebook. All the 'friends' I have are on here. There aren't many but I can separate them from the real thing, so why can't I do that with him?

After an hour or so of messing around on social media, his green light shows up, telling me he's online. My name online is a play on my surname and my profile picture is a meme so he hasn't seen a picture of me. I hover the cursor over his name in the chat section.

A message pops up... from him.

Ash: For a million pound would you eat a bowl of fried tarantula's?

Despite myself, I smile. I have no idea how this game started between us but it's one we play regularly. I smile because this game has pulled me from some of my darkest depths. I smile because it means he's thinking of me, having no idea I'm right next door to him.

So close, yet still so far.

Me: Easy money. Give me something hard.

He messages back right away.

Ash: For a mil would you send me a pic?

I grin as I instantly type: **I don't do dick pics!**

He starts typing back. I can't wait for his reply.

Ash: I love how you don't question if I'm good for the money.
He adds laughing face emoji's.

Me: I love how you don't question if I really am a dude.

He doesn't reply straight away so I start chewing my thumb, I really want to peek into the living room and watch him. Instead, I log in on my phone and take a selfie. I crop it so only my lips are visible and send it using the app. My picture pops up on the message section on my laptop and facebook says he's typing back.

Ash: I don't have a mil! Can I pay some other way?

Me: Yes! I'll let you know when I'm ready to collect...

I close my laptop and tiptoe to the door. His overnight guest must be gone if he's sat messaging me, I can't hide forever so I pull it open cautiously and walk into the living room. He still isn't fully dressed and is sprawled out on the sofa, laptop resting on his lap exactly the same as I was a few moments ago. He's smiling at the screen and I hope it's because of my messages. He looks up as I walk in and sits up patting the settee for me to sit next to him.
I sit at the opposite end and fiddle with my hands.
"I don't even know your name." he says
"It's Feli... Fliss."

"Nice to meet you Fliss. I guess from the ad you already know I'm Ash?"

I nod because my mouth won't speak.

"So, can we start again? I'm sorry about earlier but can't say that it will be the last time you'll be faced with women, usually in the morning, you think you can handle that?"

I nod again, wringing my fingers even harder.

"Do you have a boyfriend?"

My head snaps up. No beating around the bush, no easing in gently with his new flatmate, straight to the personal stuff. My mind automatically screams *Yes, it's you!* But my mouth verbalises "What? Why?"

"Just wondering if you'll be having a guy over regularly, we might have to set up a system." He muses, his finger running over his lip as he suggests it. I stare at the movement.

"No, I don't. I'm free."

"Free instead of single? Interesting choice of words." He grins

"They mean the same thing." I protest

"Do they?" he challenges

"Do you have a girlfriend?" I blurt, desperate to guide the conversation away from me but in my next breath also dreading the answer he might give.

He laughs. A real throaty belly laugh, as if I just asked the funniest question in the world. I feel my cheeks flame in embarrassment.

When he finishes he studies me, laughter lines etched around his eyes. He pauses as though he's weighing up his answer. When he speaks it's to ask a question, "Why would I *need* a girlfriend?"

"Well, no-one *needs* one, but most people *want* a significant other."

"Why?" he frowns

"Why not?" I shoot back

He grins "I think I'm going to enjoy debating with you, Fliss."

"I think you'll be disappointed, Ash."

His eyes flicker with amusement and I realise I'm enjoying this exchange as much as he appears to be. This is the part of him I get to experience online and now I'm seeing flashes of it in person.

"You remind me of someone." He says wistfully

"Someone annoying?" I joke

"I wouldn't say annoying but definitely frustrating."

"I'm glad I'm making such a good first impression."

"Your first impression was fine, the second was even better." He flashes a grin at me again and I squirm inside when I notice he has dimples. *Lord help me. Not dimples.*

"Okay, well... good. I guess I'm going to go to bed."

"Already?"

"Yes, I uh... I don't sleep very well so try and get an early start to make the most of as many hours as I can." *Plus, if I stay any longer my tongue is going to end up either licking your cheek or being just plain stuck in those indentations.*

"Let me know if you need me." He says to my retreating back, and I know if I turned around he'd be wearing that smug grin again.

Chapter 4

Felicity

Current mood – Mortified
Regret level – 10/10

I wake up the following day and stretch out as is my morning custom. I slept well considering I haven't slept in a single bed since I was a child. I roll over and quickly switch from content to disoriented, not because I'm in a new place but an even newer place.

This is not my new bedroom.

For starters I'm in a double bed, my new room has a single and my room, hopefully, doesn't smell manly, this one does. It doesn't matter that the scent smells divine, I'm on high alert as I convince myself to open my eyes and when I do I jump out of my skin as Ash is sitting next to me, fully clothed, holding out a mug of something steaming.

Just staring. At me.

I automatically pull the covers up to my chin and as I do I'm horrified to realise I'm naked. Completely and utterly starkers. He doesn't speak but the corners of his lips tip up in a supressed smile. His gorgeous eyes sparkling with mischief and a hint of secrets only he's privy to. *Has he been watching me sleep?*

"Take it." He says, pushing the mug towards me "I won't bite."

This is a dream. *It has to be.* I mean it's the most logical explanation.

"Are you actually awake this time?" he asks

"Huh?"

He clicks his fingers in front of me and I blink rapidly "Fliss, are you awake?"

"Yes." I answer in annoyance "Why are you being weird?"

He bursts out laughing, the mug I still haven't taken from him shaking along with him.

"You win on the weird front, Fliss. Was my bed comfortable?"

Oh Shit! Ignorance is all I have to offer. I clutch the quilt to me tighter, my knuckles turning white from the death grip I have on the only thing hiding my modesty. "Why am I in your bed? Did you drug me or something?" I accuse only half seriously.

"Or something." He mutters, his expression changing from playful to pissed off.

"Can you ever give a straight answer. What the hell is going on? Why am I naked?" *Please for the love of all things holy tell me he hasn't seen me naked.* Tell me I didn't have sex with the guy of my dreams and not remember it.

"Yeah, that surprised me too."

"Ash!" I yell impatiently even though I already know the answer.

He takes a deep breath as he ponders how to tell fill me in on how this mortifying situation came about. "Do you have a tendency for sleepwalking at all?"

I groan at the confirmation as I bury myself beneath the covers. I'll never shake the hue of embarrassment that floods my entire body. Avoidance is all I can rely on. I'll hide until the problem goes away.

Hiding.

In Ash's bed.

Naked.

Even in sleep, my mind, my body took me to him. Betrayed by my own traitorous body. Before, back home I could indulge in my dreams, secure in the knowledge that he was far away. Unobtainable. Of all the problems I thought I'd encounter by coming here, my sleepwalking wasn't one of them. It never factored. But then I was never supposed to move in with him. It was truly the least of my worries and concerns but right now with it smacking me in the face, giving me no alternative but to confront it I want to become invisible. Like I've always been. I want to be back in my lonely cocoon where humiliating situations such as this would never come to fruition.

"You know, Fliss, you've got some nerve presuming I did something wrong. I'm the innocent that was molested while I slept."

Yep. I'm never coming out. I feel myself sink below the covers again in complete humiliation. *Is it possible to die from embarrassment?* Because it seems like a good get out clause at this moment. I'll just die here slowly, painfully.

The top of the covers are yanked from my death grip and my face exposed. "No point hiding now. I've seen all there is to see." He grins.

My hands fly to my face, covering my eyes, "Oh God. What did we do?"

"We?! Let's get something straight right now. If something had happened *between us*, you'd most definitely remember."

"So, we... we never..." I gulp when he just stares at me as I struggle to say the words.

"We never what, Fliss?" he smirks, silently daring me to finish that sentence, so I change direction instead as I press my eyelids closed "What did I do, Ash?" I plead.

"Let's see. I woke up to my naked roommate leaning over me as if she was ready to smother me. Not in my top ten of ways to be woken I might add. When I tried to cover up your modesty like the saintly gent I am you shrieked at me like a banshee and then proceeded to try and rescue me from my evidently killer bed. You're quite strong, Fliss." He takes a sip from the mug "I guess you could say you wrestled me to the ground, then covered me with your body..." he air quotes with his fingers "... to save me. From what, you wouldn't say. Then you climbed into my bed and started snoring."

My eyes fly open "I do not snore!" I shout out far too high pitched for this time of the morning.

"Really? Out of all I just said you're going to protest over snoring?" he chuckles "And, so like the gentleman I am, I allowed you to steal my bed while I slept in yours. And I barricaded myself in." he adds pointedly.

"Ash... I..."

"And you had the cheek to moan about me walking around in my boxers yesterday. You're all front, Fliss." His eyes flick down to where my breasts are hiding under the covers. Damn him and his double meaning.

"I'm so sorry..."

"So, were you sleepwalking or was this your attempt at seducing me?"

"No! Sleepwalking, definitely sleepwalking."

"Again, with the horrified tone. You can't blame a guy for thinking that."

"No, I'm not... I don't... I... ugh, can we do this when I'm dressed, please?"

"Flustered, Fliss? I mean, I've seen it all now..."

"Okay, I get it. Enough already. *Please.* Last night was clearly embarrassing for both of us, me more so but stop dragging it out."

"Okay, since you asked so nicely."

I breathe a sigh of relief until he continues, "Although... I can't help wondering what would have happened if I had a woman in bed with me. Would you have tried to 'save' her too or would I have witnessed a nude ladies wrestling match? It's definitely something I'll dream about." He smiles

I slap his arm playfully "I would've saved her over you."

He holds his palm over his chest in mock pain "Drink this, get dressed. I'll see you when you're done." He places the mug on his bedside unit and walks out leaving me to groan my frustration. My first night here and I showcase my sleepwalking abilities. Great. And I know I didn't go to bed naked which means I stripped off before I got to him, I'll have to glue my pyjamas on tonight. Maybe chain myself to my bed.

Ash has seen me naked.

And I wasn't lucid enough to see if he appreciated what he saw. He took the greatest of joy in dragging out my embarrassment, talk about mortified. Even though he ribbed me, he was actually pretty nice natured over it. I'm not sure if the tables were turned if I'd be as understanding and accepting.

I sink back under the covers and smile to myself. *I'm in Ash's bed.*

It may be sooner than I thought and not in the way I hoped but who cares?

Certainly not me.

Ashton

Is this chick crazy? If I didn't need the financial support she offers then I might think twice about this arrangement. I should have thought it through before, but I had more pressing matters to attend to. Having a sleepwalking stranger in my apartment wasn't on the agenda. Sure it helps that she's more than fucking easy on the eye but I'm not up for another special brand of crazy. Cammy already gave me more than my fair share of that. I practically shit myself when I was yanked from sleep to her muttering incoherently, looking like a zombie straight from the nightmare I was already having and trying to drag me from my bed. Her ridiculously long blonde locks flailing like Medusa snakes. *Who knows what other shit she's capable of?* Talk about lasting first impressions. She seems sweet, innocent even, but I'm well aware appearances can be deceptive. All the stranger danger lessons my parents imparted to me were clearly for nothing. I moved this woman in based on nothing more than looks, desperation and ready money. The perfect recipe for disaster. She could be a psychopath for all I know and I've just let her into my life, my home and already my bed.

Good work Ash!

Felicity

Current mood – Nervous
Regret level - High

After stealing one of his T-shirts and darting from his room to mine I finally pluck up the courage to go and face him, this time armed with my onesie, not only is it ridiculously warm and comfortable but it practically covers every inch of my body. I'm using it as armour, but then I falter like the wuss I am and fire up my laptop instead. Rehashing what happened last night is definitely something that can wait. Just thinking about it gives me goosebumps.

I have a new message and just know it's from him before I open it.

Ash: I've found that inspiration I was searching for. The next instalment will be making its way to you quicker than I thought.

Me: Yay! Can't wait. What happened to your brick wall?

Ash: Let's just say someone smashed through it! I think my new roommate will be a great motivation to get it finished.

Bastard! He's using me for his storytelling? I start typing out a scathing reply and then remember he doesn't know I'm the same person he speaks to daily online. I still haven't quite figured out how to extricate myself from this situation. Being honest is clearly the best option but then it's over. I'll be labelled a nut job, kicked out on the street and with nowhere else to turn be forced to go back home. Back to the life I desperately need a retreat from. I bite my thumbnail as I try to figure out what to say.

Before I can come up with a response there's a rap on my door followed by "Fliss, you going to hide all day? I know women take an obscene amount of time getting ready, but this is excessive."

I roll my eyes and stick my tongue out at the door. I never realised how annoying he is. And that's the beauty of a computer screen. We can imagine what we like about the people we talk to. I built up an image of him that as yet he isn't living up to. I thought he was the strong, silent type with a playful side that needed gentle coaxing. *How wrong was I?*

"Yeah, coming." I yell in defeat.

"Really? Well, don't rush that. I'll wait 'til you're done." I swear I can hear his smile through the amused tone.

I wish I was confident enough to play him at his own game. I'd love to have the balls to pretend I was having an intense orgasm whilst screaming his name and watch how quickly the shock shuts him up, but I don't because this might be the new me but even I have some limits, or is it morals?

Instead, I swing the door open and flash him a brilliant fake smile. I spent ages back home perfecting which was my best side and I use it now.

"I think we need to sort out some house rules," I say

"I couldn't agree more." He pauses and steps back, looking me up and down, a frown creeping over his features "What the fuck are you wearing?" he chuckles

I look down at my all in one wear and cross my arms over my chest "What?" I protest "It's comfy."

"It looks like you've shit yourself and have four dicks!"

My cheeks flame, "Does not!" I protest. The truth in his statement is not something I'll own.

"Keep living in denial, Fliss. Why you want to hide those curves is up to you... but, it does look like you've crapped in it."

I walk past him and try to change the subject "Back to this list." I say hoping this steers him away from my clothing choice "Maybe we should keep our opinions to ourselves."

"I think top of the list is that we don't violate the other's privacy." The sarcasm couldn't be any thicker if he tried.

We walk over to the breakfast bar and take seats opposite each other. It feels like we're about to engage in a verbal game of chess.

"Bedrooms are out of bounds. Agreed."

"Wait." He says wandering to a drawer and coming back with a pad and pen "Probably best to jot these down, in case *someone* forgets."

I can't believe I ever thought that if my plan worked I'd give myself away by staring at him endlessly like a lovesick puppy. Looks aside, because yeah his looks are pretty damn insane but all I feel like doing is slapping him upside his head. Why does he have to be so annoying whilst still causing butterflies to dance in my belly?

"No nakedness!" I add

His eyebrows shoot up in surprise and then he's bloody grinning again "What, like ever?" he asks "Might make some things... difficult. And, really I think that rule should only apply to you." As soon as he finishes, he frowns as though he can't quite believe he said that. My body heats and tingles but at the same time, I bristle. "Oh, and don't even think about introducing that ..." he gestures with his hand at my onesie "... as preferable wear over nakedness."

I feel myself blush furiously but manage to bite back "No going to bed naked and I don't want to have to see any naked women wandering around either."

"But..."

"Don't," I warn, knowing he was going to make some reference to me being the wandering naked woman.

"No being bossy."

"No being annoying." I counter

Despite myself, I feel my lips curving into a smile. He smiles too as though the ice hadn't already officially been broken. We're acting more like brother and sister squabbling than the innocent girl and the supposed man of her dreams. We make an unspoken truce and jot down a few more ridiculous rules that we think of on the fly and pin the list to the fridge so we can add to it at a moment's notice.

"So, plans for today?" he asks

"No plans, I was just going to wing it, you?"

"This can be our bonding day then."

"Our what?"

"I think we're going to become great friends, Fliss but to do that we have to get to know one another – today, we bond."

"Why does that sound so creepy?"

"Bond, bonding, not bondage." He smiles

I slap his arm playfully "Maybe we should add no innuendos to our list?"

"I'm fluent in innuendo's, take that from me and I'd never be able to talk."

"Perfect." I smile as I realise how much I liked him when he was nothing more than a smiling profile picture "You can just sit and look pretty." I feel my face drop the moment those words come out and his face breaks into the best smile I've seen from him yet.

"I'm starting to like when you catch yourself off guard, Fliss."

"Yeah, I bet." I mumble "I didn't think you'd appreciate being classed as a pretty boy."

"Boy, no. Man, I'll take. A compliment is a compliment and it came from you so I'll allow it."

I roll my eyes. Partly at him and partly at myself. I'm worn out and the day has only just begun.

"How does our bonding session start?"

He grins "So forward, Fliss. I like it."

"Do you know how to be serious?" I ask, genuinely interested.

"Depends what task I'm being serious at. Some things I take very seriously, for example..."

I hold my hand up, "Okay! I don't need a list."

"You seem like a list person."

"Are you trying to say I'm boring?"

He laughs "See, we're finding out so much about one another already."

"Good dodge, Ash!"

"It's not the first time I've had to side-step a loaded question."

I sit down on his settee and curl my legs beneath me. "Soo, what do you want to do?"

He sits opposite me "Well, in the short space of time I've known you, you've been very revealing." He grins and runs his eyes over my body. I'm never going to live down my naked sleep-walking. "But that was just surface stuff." He continues and my face burns.

"So, I want to find out what's underneath. Go deeper." His eyes sparkle as he taunts me with his double meanings.

I'm squirming, burning and trying not to look into his eyes as he toys with me, but I know looking away will give him some satisfaction, knowing he's getting to me.

"How deep?" I ask and chalk a point to myself as his lip quirks.

"As deep as you're willing to go."

"I'm game."

Before we can continue a sharp knock on the front door has us both snapping our heads that way. I freeze as Ash creeps towards it and peers through the spyhole.

"Shit!" he hisses, turning back to me and giving my cow onesie the once over through narrowed eyes. I shrink into myself, suddenly self-conscious once again.

"It's my parents." He whispers, and my heart crashes. My potential future parents-in-law are feet away and first impressions are everything. I glance down at the udder on my onesie on full display and a nervous giggle at my choice of outfit slips out.

Ash shakes his head at me in disbelief and on a deep breath opens the door.

A large man, easily past 6-foot tall walks in, nodding to Ash and slapping him on his back as he passes. I can see nothing else as he stops in his tracks when he notices me. I don't know how to react and he seems lost too, so I stand up and watch his eyes flick to my cow udders, my face burns as I walk forward unsurely and offer an outstretched, sweaty hand.

He turns away from me before seeing my gesture and speaks to his wife.

"He has company." He tells her

I let my hand drop to my side and discreetly wipe it in my onesie just as his mother appears before me, the picture of sophistication in a white blouse, fitted black trousers, and a delicate silver necklace. Her dark hair is pulled back in a classic updo and I stare at her, now understanding where Ash gets his looks from.

"How lovely to meet you...?" she says

"Felicity." I offer "Lovely to meet you too."

"What an interesting outfit." She smiles, and there's no hint of sarcasm, she's trying to make me feel comfortable and I could hug her for that alone.

"I'll leave you to it." I direct at Ash.

"No, please, sit with us. We don't get to meet many of Ashton's friends. Don't leave on our account." His mum says as she takes a seat at the breakfast bar.

I look at Ash and he just shrugs, resigned to the fact that I won't be escaping.

"Fliss is my new roommate." He tells his parents but looks pointedly at his dad as he says it.

"Oh." His mum utters, a hint of disappointment in her words.

"Well, I'm glad you took my advice, son." His father responds

"You didn't tell us." His mum scolds

"It just happened a day ago, mum. I wanted Fliss to have a chance to settle in before you mothered her."

"I would not." She protests "Though why you think having a mother that cares is so awful I'll never know. When I'm gone you'll miss my mothering."

And for the first time since this crazy plan was put into action, I miss my parents. *The people who raised me.* I feel the tears threatening to spill and clear my throat in the hopes they'll go away. I miss my mother's mothering, she often made me feel stifled as she was so overprotective but she was my mum and every girl needs their mum.

"Fliss, are you okay?" Ash asks, appearing at my side and taking my arm

I nod and manage to whisper "Excuse me for a moment." I push back the kitchen stool and make a beeline to my room.

Chapter 5

Ashton

"I like that you had the sense to room share with a female that clearly isn't trying to get in your pants." My dad says as he takes the seat Fliss just ran from.

"Dad!" I snap "Why do you say that?"

"Oh come on son, I know you think you're god's gift but look at her, she's adorably cute but slobbing around in a most unbecoming outfit, no makeup... she's not exactly making an effort to catch your attention like most of the women you entertain."

"I like that about her."

"Me too." My mother agrees

"It was a compliment." He mutters

"Yeah, a backhanded one." I point out

He sighs as he walks over to my fridge and helps himself to a can of coke, "So, where'd you find her?" Dad asks

"Oh you know, the street corner."

"Ashton!" My mother snaps as my father sighs

"She saw the ad, arranged a meet and that was it," I tell him

"What does she do?"

I feel my brow wrinkle as I think back to if she told me her job. I shrug when I realise I have no idea.

"You don't know do you?" dad accuses "You got taken in by a pretty face, how do you know she can even pay her way? Our deal still stands, son."

"Yes, I'm well aware of the deal, dad. You ram it down my throat at every opportunity. She paid a month upfront, she's not going to take me for a free ride, so don't worry."

"I'm glad that free rides are a thing of the past. Maybe now you'll value money a little bit more."

"Grey!" My mum warns as she lightly slaps his arm "We didn't come here to give him an inquisition. He's doing what you asked so lay off, please."

"Why did you come over?" I ask

Mum snaps her head in my direction "Can I not visit my only child without there being an ulterior motive?"

"Not usually," I mutter

"Just checking you're still alive seeing as you don't answer my calls or visit us." She says as her eyes well with tears and I'm smacked in my gut with guilt. I go to her and hug her "I'm sorry mum. I've been busy with work, it's no excuse I know but you know once I start I get lost in my own world."

My dad snorts and I know it's over my use of the word 'work'. He's not exactly supportive of my passion, especially as so far it hasn't paid well. With my first book, I queried a ton of agents to secure a publishing deal and was rejected by all. I'm now exploring the self -publishing route which is more work, though I'm also hoping it'll be more beneficial.

His business is all about making money. Therefore, he judges one's worth on their bank balance. His construction business has done well over the years and he's yearning for me to join. So he's cut me off, starting with the apartment. Originally it was 'bought for me' but since I told him I'd be starting a career as a writer that changed to it's for me to 'rent' from him, hence the need for my roommate otherwise I'd never afford this place off my savings alone. Dad's ultimatum has caused a rift between my parents as mum hates seeing me struggle when they're loaded. I happen to disagree, I'm an adult, I shouldn't be relying on my parents for everything and having to step up and take responsibility for the first time in my life for everything is somewhat freeing. I like not being beholden to my father, it seems he's the one struggling to cope now he's loosened the reins because he has nothing to hold over me.

That's the funny thing about parents, mine anyway – they spend so many years raising you, providing for everything you need, nourishing and protecting you that when the time comes and they're left with an empty nest they don't know how to process it. They're not equipped to deal with the feeling of being unneeded, however untrue that is, they still feel it. They manifest ways to keep you under their wings, for us it's stifling but for them, I guess it's a coping mechanism for their new life with only one another. It's a task I don't envy my mother. My dad's real name isn't Grey, it's a nickname his mates bestowed on him before I was even born. Grey as in the colour or in his case his mood. They always said he was old before his time, he was always driven to make something better of his life and with that stead-fast determination his demeanor was often unapproachable and 'grey'.

Mum pulls away from my hug and gives dad a warning glare. "How is the new book going, Ashton?"

"Slowly." I tell her "I'd hit a wall but I think I'm finally getting there."

"What's it about?" she continues and I'm grateful for her interest.

"You don't want to know, Mum." I chuckle

"Great." Dad says "He's writing smut. I'm so proud."

"Well, I aim to displease, dad. You know that."

We engage in a stare-off, neither of us willing to back down.

"Just stop, both of you." Mum demands "Can you start acting like father and son again instead of strangers. I'm sick and tired of it. I didn't come here to watch you engage in another pissing contest." I smirk, my mother rarely swears and like a child, whenever she slips up it amuses me. She muffles a theatrical sob with her hand before leaving the kitchen, pecking me on the cheek and then turning back to us briefly she announces "I'm leaving, I'll wait for you in the car."

Dad makes a hasty retreat not long after mum, for some reason it's hard for us to be alone together, awkward. I don't recall when that started but I do know it hasn't always been this way between us. After he left I immediately felt the tension in my shoulders ease. I tried writing again but couldn't get into it. I released my first book 6 months ago and it was pretty well received going off my expectations which was for it to be a flop. I haven't raked in the money from sales but at least I'm making sales. I even gained a few fans or followers and managed to snag myself a beta reader for the book I'm currently struggling with.

I check in with my mate Trina to make sure she's doing better today and then mess around on social media but the one person who'd make me feel better isn't online, my mystery friend has been uncharacteristically AWOL and I'm feeling her absence more than I do my real life in the flesh friends. I decide now is the right time to check on Fliss. Or as I now know – Felicity. Maybe she can cheer me up. And more importantly, my decisive action of just moving her in from our first meet wasn't a smart move. I was desperate and would have accepted anyone as long as they had the first-month's rent upfront. I know nothing about my new roommate apart from the fact that she sleepwalks and I know I need to find out if this is going to be a long term arrangement or if I'll be back to square one pretty quickly money wise. Time to grill Fliss and get to know her.

"Felicity!" I sing-song outside her door, followed by an unnecessary Bang, bang, bang.

She opens it with red-rimmed eyes but tries to hide her sadness with a hint of a smile. "Ashton?"

I notice that she's upset because she uses my full name. Her sad smile and soft tone of voice make me think she's trying to hide her unhappiness.I won't broach the subject. Instead, I grin "I just wanted to try it out. I'll revert back to Fliss if you go back to calling me Ash. Deal?"

"Hmmm, I think I prefer Ashton." she teases.

"Our bonding sesh was cut short. Fancy revisiting it?"

"Sure, *Ashton*." She smiles and walks past me. I'm about to check her out when I realise she's still wearing that ridiculous cow onesie and I can't make out fuck all of her body. She may have been naked last night but it was stupidly dark and I was in a state of shock. Then I remember, I can't fuck this up. Lusting over my flatmate is plain stupid. I can't mess around with her, there'll be no dabbling because I can't afford to cause any kind of resentment between us. I need her to stay. And if I screw with her there's a chance she'll leave, and I'll be back to square one. I can't think with my dick.

I follow after her and find she's made herself comfortable on the corner settee. I think about throwing myself down right next to her, when we're in close proximity she always blushes and I enjoy knowing I cause it. I enjoy watching it spread from her cheeks down her neck. She's affected by me and knowing a woman finds you attractive is good for the ego. I wisely opt to sit as far away as possible, reminding myself of my no games rule. And giving her a moment to compose herself. I might be a wind up but even I can see something has rattled her and being myself right now would be unfair on her fragile emotions.

She looks up at me, expectantly, hesitantly and there it is... the blush. I guess I don't need to be all over her personal space to make it happen. I watch it spread, following its path with my eyes. Making her wait. She starts to fidget under my scrutiny and for some reason watching her squirm thrills me.

Flatmate.

She's just your flatmate I remind myself.

"So, Fliss. Where shall we start?"

"I don't know. You're the one that wanted to bond. I thought you'd have it all planned out."

She maintains eye contact for a split second before shrugging in feigned disinterest but she's fooling no one.

"I'm sorry about my parents, if they made you uncomfortable..."

"That's not why I left, Ash." She interrupts "I... I just thought you could do with some privacy. That's all." Her head drops again and I know that was a blatant lie but instead of calling her on it I let it slide.

"Privacy? No. Next time stick around, you can be my armour. With you to focus on I'll be left well alone." I smile at her as she looks at me from under her lashes. "Anyway, enough about the parentals, this is our bonding time. I want to know all about you Fliss...?"

"Montgomery." She fills for me

"Felicity Montgomery." I frown as I test the name on my lips and my head tries to wrap around why it sounds so familiar, but I can't put my finger on it. "It's pretty. Suits you."

She smiles and I take note of how it lights up her whole face. A real, genuine, unguarded smile from Fliss is a sight to behold.

"Before we start, how about some food? Fuel for our bonding time?"

"Sounds good, I'm starving." She replies

"So, do you cook?" I raise a hopeful brow

She shakes her head on a small smile "If you were hoping for a flat mate that would cook for you, you're going to be disappointed. I'm capable of many things, cooking isn't one of them."

Capable of many things... "I *need* many things, Fliss, a cook isn't one of them."

"Touche."

"Before I start on the food, give me a hint, tell me just one of your hidden talents."

She scrunches her nose as she wonders what information to part with and then her eyes light up as she faces me fully. She holds up one finger as she says "Sono in grado di parlare in 5 lingue diverse."

I don't know what she said, but she has my attention. Listening to a woman speak in another language is sexy as hell. Before I can ask what she said, she holds up a second finger "Kann ich 5 verschiedene Sprachen sprechen."

Again, I have no idea what the language is or what she said, but I'm hooked. This one was different to the first and doesn't sound as sexy. That's when I twig why she's holding up fingers, 2 for 2 languages she's fluent in.

She holds up the other 3 fingers and in quick succession recites "Yo hablo 5 idiomas diferentes, Je parle 5 langues différentes, Eu posso falar 5 línguas diferentes." She sits back beaming from ear to ear.

I recognise the French and 5 has been in every sentence along with the finger clues. I figure she's been repeating 'I speak 5 languages' or something to that effect.

"I'm impressed, I can barely speak one." I tell her.

"Once you've learnt two, picking up anymore is pretty easy. I can teach you if you like?" she blushes at her offer as though she's being presumptuous.

"Deal, if I can teach you how to cook?"

"It's about time someone did." She murmurs "You're on."

"What languages were they, by the way? I figured French, but what about the others?"

"German, Spanish, Portuguese and Italian."

"So technically you're fluent in 6?"

"Yeah, I guess. I want to learn more though, some of them just won't stick."

"It's pretty cool to know as many as you do, was there a reason for learning them?"

"Not really, not to start with anyway. My Parents wanted me to learn as much as possible, knowing other languages seemed to make sense and once I started I toyed with the idea of becoming a translator but... well, life had other ideas for me." She shrugs and starts picking at her onesie.

"You're in charge, y'know... of your future I mean. My parents had hopes for me but I settled for disappointing them in order to follow my own dreams. They'll get over it eventually, I wouldn't have got over not trying to achieve what I wanted. You just need to weigh up what you want and need versus those around you."

She nods as she plays with a tendril of hair "You're right, Ash. Baby steps though."

Chapter 6

Felicity

Current mood – Comfortable
Regret level - 0

Two weeks have passed since our bonding day. Two blissful weeks. Weeks that I'll remember and treasure forever. I managed to maintain my cover and not give myself away by telling as much of the truth as possible. Half-truths. I told him I've taken over the family business which luckily for me is quite lucrative hence having no real need to work. I'm a wealthy woman which I didn't divulge but having money has made this pipe dream possible. He knows I'm an only child as is he and he told me he writes (which I already knew).

Living with Ash is hard work. He's effortlessly sexy, funny and a natural flirt. It's like he can't help himself. I've learned so much about him. Nothing big. But all the quirks he has that make us all individual. Little things, like he stirs his coffee precisely eight times before he'll drink it. He likes sweets a lot, but never eats the green ones. Sometimes we'll be mid-conversation and he wanders away in his mind. I've figured that this happens when an idea hits him or a line for his story needs to be jotted down. We often spend our time in companionable silence – him writing his story and me updating my journal. Only yesterday he stopped writing, looked at me over the top of his screen and asked: "Do you keep a diary?"

"I suppose so." I told him "Though I don't think of it as one."

"Why are you always writing in it?"

"So I never forget a single experience," I replied truthfully.

I went back to updating it but could feel him watching me. I knew he wanted to ask more and was battling with himself how far to push me for insight into my life. After a few minutes he went back to his story and I released a thankful breath of relief.

I've never felt this comfortable in my own skin, never felt this kind of contentment and peace. He's quite simply easy to be around. Life feels effortless with him. This feels like it was meant to be. Living together has slotted into our lives with such ease, maybe it's the familiarity we already have from speaking online, even if he's unaware of it. But we gel, we hit it off in person as much as we did from behind a screen.

Despite his suggestion when I first moved in, he hasn't had a woman here once. It could be because I've monopolised his time, ensuring he stayed in with me every night just hanging out, it could be because he just isn't interested in getting laid or it could be because spending time with me is more preferable. I like to think it's the latter.

My favourite part of living with him is every morning after his shower I wander in the bathroom for mine to find he's drawn a smiley face on the mirror from the steam. The first time I noticed it I spent an age just standing there staring at it. I look forward to these shower smileys every morning, it might be silly but it means he's thinking about me... I hope. Now, I don't know if he's always done that or if he does it for my benefit, maybe it's how he always started his days before I came along, but it's cute and endearing and something I'll sorely miss when I have to leave.

Ash is a tactile being, so innocently touchy-feely. He loves holding hands, hugging and holding me when we watch films. He's thoughtful, always considering and taking into account my feelings.

I've fallen harder than I ever could have imagined.

I've fallen harder than I ever should have allowed myself to.

He's also ridiculously upbeat. Seriously, it's like the guy never has a down day, even when he's at fifty-percent he's still happier and perkier than most human beings.

He makes me laugh. I can't remember the last time I laughed before meeting him. It's been a while. A long while. I'm completely and utterly addicted to how he makes me feel. It's a feeling I don't want to give up.

It makes me feel awful for continuing to lie to him because everything he'd told me online about himself is true. He hasn't deceived me at all, not once and I just keep adding to my ever-growing lie list. I can't find a way to now drop it on him. So I'm praying that the longer I'm around and the more attached he gets to me or the more indispensable I make myself, when the time comes he'll weigh up the pro's and con's and decide to keep me around anyway. *Denial is my friend.*

"Fliss!" he hollers

"Yeah?" I yell back

"First cooking lesson in five minutes, be ready." He says

Exactly five minutes later, we're stood side by side in the kitchen. Ash is a stickler for timekeeping.

"Is there anything you've always wanted to learn to cook or shall we just start with basics?"

"Cake. I need to learn how to make cakes."

"I was thinking proper food. Cooking as opposed to baking."

"Oh come on. Both options include ingredients, right? Plee-assse?" I beg and dramatically flutter my eyelashes

"Cake it is."

I smile widely and watch his eyes fall to my lips, they linger for a moment before he clears his throat and turns to start gathering items and ingredients.

He starts adding ingredients to a metal bowl, explaining about quantities as he does before giving me the task of breaking eggs into it. Instead of tapping against the bowl, I more or less smash it against the side causing egg and shell to all make it into the mix.

He looks horrified for a second before he bursts out laughing "Jesus, Fliss, you're dangerous."

"There's no way I can fish out all those shell bits, let's start from scratch." He throws the lot into the bin, cleans the bowl and starts again, this time I'm allowed to measure the flour because any idiot can pour and count, right?

"How come you're fluent in many languages but can't even work an egg?"

"Shh, I'm concentrating," I tell him as I keep tipping the flour

"Do you know how to do toast?" he continues with his familiar smirk

"Yes, the toaster takes care of that for me."

"Right, I'll add the eggs, pay attention." He tells me

I roll my eyes but still I lean closer to see how this is done. He cracks first one then two effortlessly, the egg slips out as the shell remains in his palm.

"Now you mix." He says

I start mixing as he potters around, washing utensils, checking the oven and then he's behind me, leaning over my shoulder as he inspects my handiwork. He presses up closer and I bite my lip before realising I've stopped moving. The mixture is no longer being mixed but my damn emotions are.

He grabs both of my pigtails, pulling them gently so they hang down my back instead of my front "These should be tied back."

"They are." I protest

He shakes his head "I don't like hair in my food."

"Well tuck them in my onesie then." I tell him as my hands are covered in allsorts and I'm not getting it in my hair.

Instead he pulls out each pony, gathering my hair into a bunch at the back of my neck, he tugs again like he's testing something out and then I feel him sectioning it. He hums as he braids my hair and it's the most surreal thing I've ever witnessed. I can't even braid, so the fact he can is astonishing to me. Having his hands in my hair is just a bonus. But every time his fingers graze my neck, I tingle all the way down my spine.

"It's lumpy." He breathes against my ear once he's finished with my unruly locks.

I start up my mixing again, pretending I'm composed as he just watches "It's meant to be a smooth texture." He continues.

"Maybe if you weren't pressed up against me, I'd be able to get the job done." I breathe out.

He pushes in closer, boxing me in against him and the unit. I take a deep breath before jutting my arse out, pushing right against his crotch. I hear him suck in a breath and count this as being even.

He spins me to face him "Am I distracting you, Fliss?"

"Yes."

"I like when you're distracted by me. I like even more when I'm distracted by you."

I stare into his eyes trying to decipher what he's up to. "Yeah? Well when I'm learning, I like to concentrate. Distractions aren't appreciated." I bring my hand up as though I'm about to gently touch his face and then with my free hand reach behind me, dip it in the bag of flour still sat on the side and smear it all over his cheek.

He steps back as I do a little triumphant jig at the shock on his face. He was winding me up on purpose, as though he knows the effect he has on me. Well, that showed him. I'm not putty, even in his hands.

"You want to play, Fliss?" he all but growls

Uh oh, I don't mind dishing it out but no way do I want to be on the receiving end. I shake my head slightly as I chew my bottom lip. He pulls my lip free, comes to stand beside me while my heart hammers in my chest, waiting for what he's about to do.

But nothing happens, no retribution, he starts mixing the mixture, continuing my cooking lesson in his usual carefree way, explaining things to me, until it's being spooned into a cake tray.

"Now for the best part." He says, his eyes shining

"The best part is eating it."

His eyes widen as he shakes his head, looking at me like I'm insane, "You're so deprived. The best part is licking the bowl and spoon."

"Why would anyone do that?" My nose wrinkles at the thought.

"Why?! Because it's awesome. I can't believe you've never done this." He shakes his head like the notion is completely crazy.

He raises the wooden spoon we've been using and before I know what's happening he's smeared the mix across my lips. Stray strands of my hair still managing to get stuck in it. This is the payback he's been waiting for. The cake tin hasn't been put in the oven yet and like a beacon beckoning me I turn to it, dunk my hand in and then run it over Ash's shell shocked face.

My hand drips mix all over the floor, so does his face. It's silent for a moment, both of us in shock, before we move simultaneously.

War breaks loose.

Flour is thrown, mixture is launched, egg and shell end up in my hair, on Ash' head and running down his face. The kitchen is a disaster as we leap out of each other's way, ducking and diving in the most enjoyable food fight there ever was. Anything and everything to hand is used in the bid to win. I grab a bottle of tomato sauce and squirt it all over him, he grabs me and pulls me against his body so that it transfers to me as well. I'm giggling, Ash is beaming and the cake is forgotten which is probably good as it's likely no longer fit for human consumption. Breathless we finally slide down to the floor, leaning against the cupboards, covered in ingredients, wearing the biggest smiles and a whole lot of mess.

We turn to look at one another, huge grins adorning our faces, acting young and carefree was a tonic I never knew I needed. Being silly and childish is something I've never had the opportunity to be. Ash leans forward, his eyes focused entirely on my lips and I register he's moving in for a kiss. I feel myself lean closer. His head dips until there's no space left between us. His lips barely brush over mine, lingering for only a moment before he runs his tongue over the seam of them and pulls back agonisingly slowly "I never got to lick the bowl, so your lips were the next best option." He winks

My lips tingle. I have to stop reaching for them and touching them. I think my heart momentarily stopped beating because now it's starting back up again and the whoosh is deafening to my ears. It was nothing, barely counts as a kiss, but to me, it was my fairy tale dream come true. I want more.

"Well, I never got to either..." I leave the unspoken question in the air, wondering if I'm being too bold.

"You're right, you missed out. How do we rectify that?" he muses, before wrapping his hand around my neck and pulling me back in as his lips crash to mine. This time he doesn't hold back. Instead of stopping this time, my heart speeds up dangerously. I'm completely consumed by this kiss, by him, as my heart hammers in my chest.

When we finally pull apart I feel my face flush, he stares at me for what feels like an eternity before jumping to his feet and starting to clean up.

I sit there for a while, delirious over what just happened and when my racing heart resumes its normal beat I also rise. Our attempt at cake making may have failed but something else was achieved. I'm gutted about the cake, though because it would go down lovely right now.

We each start the tidy up process silently and in separate sections so we can't start up again. I hop in the shower, then resign to my room for a journal update.

"Fliss." Ash calls "We're going out tonight. No arguing."

I pause mid-way through updating my journal and slam it closed. I stroll from my room to his in a few steps carrying my journal as a shield. His door is open so I just walk in, he's reclined on his bed, freshly showered, watching tv. "I'll pass, Ash. I..."

"Nope." He dismisses without even looking my way

"What do you mean – nope?"

"You're coming out. As much as I've enjoyed keeping you to myself, my friends are highly suspicious and think I've made you up. You're coming."

"You've told your friends about me?" I gasp

He turns the tv off and angles his body to face me "Why wouldn't I have?"

Oh, I don't know. Because in my fantasy land I've managed to convince myself that you also have no friends, that only you and I exist and no one can penetrate the little bubble we've created. I thought he was a fellow hermit.

"What have you told them?" I ask nervously as I fidget on the spot. Great, more people to lie to. I can hold my own on a one to one basis but including others? I'll never remember all the untruths.

His face breaks out into a wide smile and the dimples I

discovered the first week break out on his face. I love those bloody dimples, they're my weak spot for sure "This and that..."

I rub my hands over my face. I've been caught sleepwalking by him another three times since the naked incident and although those times didn't involve my nakedness, they were still pretty embarrassing. I've started to think my sleepwalking is amplified by the sheer pressure and constant worry that I'll be caught out, the guilt at being such a liar that causes me to do it even more. I also sleeptalk and am beyond scared that I'll blurt out one of my untruths whilst asleep and he'll find out.

"You didn't?" I demand

"No idea what you're on about." He smirks

"There's no way I'm coming if you've told them, Ashton!"

He barks out a laugh and my hands fly to my hips which makes him laugh even harder. I turn ready to storm out of his room.

"I haven't said a word. But if you come it'll level the playing field..."

Intrigued, I turn back around to face him "How so?"

"They have dirt on me, that I'm sure they'll be only too pleased to share. They have endless amounts of stories they can fill you in on. We'll be even on the embarrassment front."

"I doubt it." I mutter "If, and this is a big if I decide to come, where are we going and with how many of your friends?"

"It's a surprise."

"I don't like surprises."

"Wow, you're cranky when derailed from normal procedure."

"Ash, please..."

"I love when you beg, Fliss." He winks and flashes that grin at me again, distracting me with those dimples "We're just going to a bar down the street. I know how much you love your sleep... walking, so I'll have you home at a decent hour. Don't be a killjoy. Live a little."

I roll my eyes at him "Dummer idiot." I mutter before turning and stomping from his room. I hear his chuckle "I understood that one, Fliss, dumb idiot? You need to work on your insults." I make it back to mine and shut the door with a little more force than needed and hear his continued chuckling at my stroppiness. I open the door and poke my head back out "It means stupid idiot, not dumb." I close my door again ignoring him and the sound of his hysterics. It's then I realise I left without finding out numbers. How many friends will I be expected to make small talk with tonight? And what the hell do I wear? I look at the latest onesie I'm currently wearing, a fetching giraffe design and my shoulders sag.

Stupid Ash and his stupid plans!

I avoided Ash all day. I needed time to prepare, and by prepare, I mean mentally. Wisely he didn't seek me out either, he could probably sense he'd won this battle and if he wound me up it'd start a war. I chose an outfit, then another and another, until my room looked like it had been raided by the cops. I did my make up, then wiped it off, then repeated. Same with my hair. I styled it up, then down, then curled it, then straightened it. I'm bloody exhausted just from the getting ready ritual but as Ash taps on my door, I realise I'm out of time to prepare anymore. I reluctantly walk to it trying to maintain some semblance of composure when inside I'm quaking.

"Fliss, you ready?" he asks gently

I open my door as I chew on the inside of my mouth, just waiting for his scathing reaction to my outfit, which seems to be another quirk of his – mocking my clothing.

Instead, he's silent and it's something I'm so unused to I flick my eyes up to peer at him. His gaze roams all over me and I hear him inhale. I suck in a breath, preparing for the jibe that's sure to follow.

"Wow! You look... wow."

"Huh?" Slips from my lips in sheer confusion

"Is this for my benefit or my friends? Because I have to tell you, Fliss, I'm re-thinking taking you out now. Maybe we should stay in?"

"Is it that bad that you don't even want to be seen in public with me? God, Ash I tried. I'm..."

He puts his hand over my mouth and stares at me with complete sincerity "Fliss, you look amazing. Can't say I didn't love the messy food look, but this? *You* look edible. I meant that I wanted to keep you to myself. If I take you out looking like that, my mates will be hitting on you all night." His hand drops away and I mutter "Eh?"

He smiles "Not used to compliments, hey? Well, get ready because you're going to be bombarded with them tonight – maybe try 'thank you' instead of 'huh' and 'eh', just a tip." He raises his arm and gently tucks a stray lock of hair behind my ear, gazing at me as he does.

The world slows down for seconds as I'm held by those warm,

brown eyes. Something shifts, he clears his throat and holds his arm out to me so I link mine through it, feeling all the more nervous now but for completely different reasons than before. *Did we just have a moment?* My inner Fliss does a little dance and squeal. Ash likes my outfit. I heard that you couldn't go wrong with a little black dress and boy does that seem to be true. Being described as amazing and wow has me rethinking my day wear. Maybe it's time to quit with the onesies and show him I can look *wow* all the time. The effort used to seem pointless, but then I never had anyone to appreciate it before. No one who would complement and flatter me. No one I wanted to look nice for. *How else will I make him fall head over heels for me?*

We leave the flat and take a leisurely walk down the street. The air is crisp and I soak up the sensation of not only being out but at night time no less and with a boy. Ash squeezes my arm reassuringly and I swear it makes me fall for him a little harder. Beneath all the ribbing and piss taking is a genuinely decent guy.

We walk past a few shops, then take a left through an alley before coming out the other side and stopping outside a small bar.

Ash holds the door open for me and I step into bright lights, loud chatter and what sounds like karaoke. The place is packed and my nerves kick in. *New experience* I repeatedly tell myself *Embrace it.*

"You'll be fine." Ash murmurs in my ear and his breath on me makes me tingle. He snatches up my hand, entwining our fingers and starts leading me over to a table in the corner where two guys and one woman sit smiling our way.

The woman jumps up from her seat as we approach and pulls

me into an unexpected hug. My C cups squish into her neck and my face flames. Ash tries to release his hand but I hold on to it for dear life. When he manages to pry it away he circles his way around us, grinning at me as he shakes his hand out in pretend pain and lets me be manhandled by this pocket-size stranger. *Traitor.*

"It's so good to finally meet you." Strange woman says as she pulls back and studies me "We thought Ash had made you up." She laughs. "But now I see why he's kept you under lock and key. I'm Trina and I didn't know what you liked to drink so I ordered us a pitcher to share." She leads me to the table, motioning for me to slide in the booth next to Ash and then she blocks me in as she throws herself down next to me. *I'm trapped.*

"Tree, calm down. Take a breath for God's sake woman." One of the guys tells her.

She replies by flipping him off.

"Everyone, this is Fliss." Ash tells the group and they all shout their hello's to me. I smile and nod at their welcome. "Fliss, these are Jake, Nathan and Trina." He points to the two guys as he introduces them and they both grin at me. Jake is blonde and wily, his grin lop-sided. Nathan has long brown hair and looks to be of the same build as Ash, he stares at me curiously whereas Jake blatantly ogles.

"Nice to meet you all," I tell them

The guys start up a conversation between themselves, leaving me to feel like a spare part, but Trina nudges my arm and indicates the pitcher in front of her. It has two straws in it and she pushes it my way. "I'm not much of a drinker," I say honestly.

"Honey, you're going to need a drink to get through tonight.

They're leaving you alone for now but pretty soon they're gonna be all over you wanting to know the ins and outs of your life."

Before she's even finished speaking my lips wrap around the straw and suck. I've never been drunk but if that's what it takes to avoid any awkward questions that can trip me up then I'm all for it.

"Atta girl!" Trina giggles

The night rolls on by without any mishaps or overstepping, no interviewing of the new girl has taken place and I feel buzzed. If I knew alcohol created this carefree feeling I would've indulged in it a long time ago. Trina is lovely, she's bubbly and friendly but there's an edge to her, she's someone I'd love to have as a friend. She's about 5,5 and has a mass of long red hair. She's sang karaoke three times already and even though her voice is shockingly bad she gets raucous applause and doesn't seem to care how she's received because she's just enjoying herself. I've noticed Ash and the others keeping a watchful eye on her all night, it's obvious how much they care about her and I find myself wishing yet again, that I had friends, people to be important to.

She slides back in next to me and puts her mouth to my ear "I need to pee. Come with me."

She stands up and waits for me to join her but I don't know why I need to. Why does she need me to hold her hand while she pees? *Is this the norm*, what girls do? Or is she trying to save me from being left with all three guys? On that thought, I spring from my seat and follow her to the ladies.

She doesn't go into the cubicle but stands in front of the mirror reapplying her lipstick. I stand watching her. "So, how do you like living with Ash?" She asks

"So far so good." I reply

"Really?"

"Yes. It's taken a bit of getting used to living with a guy but I think we're doing okay. Why? Has he said otherwise?"

She throws her head back and laughs "It's okay, Fliss, you don't need to be so guarded. He's been pretty tight-lipped where you're concerned. I just wondered how you're putting up with him?"

"Oh." I breathe a sigh of relief "Well, he is pretty exhausting."

Her eyes twinkle "I knew it! He's got you into bed already hasn't he?"

"What?! No. I meant his personality, it's tiring just keeping up with someone so... chipper."

"Ash – chipper?" she shakes her head "Must be the effect you have on him then. He's been nothing but grim the last few months."

"Are we talking about the same guy?"

"I'm glad you're making him happy again, Fliss. Seeing him down was hard to watch."

"Why was he down?"

She turns towards me and stares as though she's trying to figure out whether she should say any more. He's her long- time friend, I'm just the girl he currently lives with. An outsider.

"Just some stuff with his parents. Not my place to say really." She shrugs like it's no big deal and resumes studying herself in the mirror.

I love how she tries to give me a heads up without betraying her loyalty to her friend. But now I'm curious.

"He's cheered me up too. So I guess we're even."

She studies me again as though she's about to ask why I was sad and then thinks better of it. There's friendly and then there's overstepping. She seems to recognise the fine line between them. Her nose crinkles and she sighs " Look Fliss, I don't want to be one of 'those' people but I need to say this, he's a good guy, one of my best friends and I know you're just flatmates but please don't let him down. He's been used enough and deserves so much more."

My heart drops because the thought of him being used and let down makes my insides contract, but also, because I know I'm about to tell another lie. "Trina, I... I have no intention of using him or hurting him or anything else you think I might do. We're friends and I don't treat my friends like that." I gulp as I realise that rolled off my tongue easier than it should have. My first lie to this woman; he's definitely going to be hurt when I finally tell him my truth and he'll definitely feel used.

She smiles like I've told her all she needed to hear, accepts it, believes my words. I've never felt shittier. "Good, now I've got that off my chest let's dance!" she says, grabbing my arm and pulling me through the door.

We return to the bar area and she makes a beeline for the dance floor, still dragging me along with her. I look over to our table and see that Ash isn't there so reluctantly allow her to manhandle me. I start swaying to the music in what I hope resembles the effortless moves Trina is pulling. She gives me a thumbs up and loses herself in the crowd of other dancers. I spin and catch Ash watching me from the bar as I sway again to the beat. He's smiling, his dimples on show and his gaze glued to me. It gives me an incentive to keep going. He's watching me dance and … liking it. *Another new experience.* Something as simple as dancing in front of others and I've never done it before. Music is supposed to be all about the rhythm so I let myself get lost in the music, lost in my own world, eyes closed enjoying this feeling.

After a few more minutes I decide to give up and walk back to the table when a hand slips around my waist making me freeze. A strong hand keeps me in place as I try to swivel and see who has hold of me. The hand starts creeping upward as I'm forced to move with whoever it is and I panic. *Is this the norm? Acceptable?* I'm like a deer in the headlights.

"Back off."

Jake appears before me and gives me a reassuring grin before fixing steely eyes back on the guy touching me. I'm released and don't even look back to see who it was before darting off to my table. I slowly lower myself to the seat and down the last drops of alcohol in the glass.

Jake joins me. "Are you okay?"

"Yes, thanks to you." I sigh. He frowns at my apparent shakiness, so I admit "I've never really been to pubs or clubs. I'm not used to drinking and I'm definitely not used to being groped."

"You've never been to clubs?"

"No."

"Wow. I don't know what to say. I don't think I've ever met someone that's never got shit faced."

"Well, now you have. Seriously, though, thank you, Jake."

"No worries. To be honest I did it to save my own skin. If anything had upset you tonight that I could've prevented Ash would skin me alive." He chuckles

I smile "Where is Ash?"

"Went to the bar and hasn't been seen since."

I look around the room desperately trying to pick him out. His space at the bar is now occupied by a hen party and he's nowhere to be seen. "Don't look so nervous." He jokes "I don't bite... Unless asked nicely." He smiles again and I feel no more at ease even though he's trying to be friendly.

"Relax Fliss, he'll be back. Gives us a chance to chat anyway. So, if you've never drunk before do I take it you've also never danced before?"

I shake my head, a blush creeping over me.

"That explains it then." He murmurs "Did you grow up in a convent or something?"

"I might as well have."

He ponders my answer for a few seconds before realising I won't be divulging any more on that subject, so he changes tact.

"What do you do, Fliss? For work?"

"I'm... a business owner I guess."

"You guess?" He quirks a brow "How can you not know if you own a business?"

"No, I do. It's not something I set up but something I inherited. I still have trouble believing it's mine."

I watch as he digests this information and I can see his cogs turning.

"How long do you plan on sticking around then? I mean can you run this business from anywhere or is it something you'll need to get back to?"

"I didn't really have a timeframe in mind to be honest. I'm taking a break and it won't fall apart without me. But I'm happy and have no plans to leave anytime soon. Unless Ash wants me to of course."

"Where did you move from?"

"London."

"So, if work wasn't the reason for your move, what brought you all the way out here?"

I stall by taking a sip of the alcohol in front of me. It's happening – the interrogation I expected but it's even worse than I imagined because he's asking me with a smile on his face, needling information in a friendly way which is all aimed to catch me off guard.

"Truthfully?" I reply

"Up to you." He replies on a shrug.

"Change of scenery. The chance to travel and be spontaneous for once in my life. I want to make memories."

He nods as though that's an acceptable answer but I'm not sure he buys it completely so I take a risk. Smiling, I lean forward and lower my voice conspiratorially "Plus, I planned to see if I could make my flatmate fall in love with me."

He laughs "I can't tell if you did go down the truthful route or not, Fliss. But either way, I wish you luck." He tips his beer towards me and I clink it with the empty pitcher.

Chapter 7

Felicity

Current mood – To be decided
Regret level – Also, to be decided

W e make it back to the apartment after what turned out to be a really good night. Ash's friends were lovely, especially Trina, who insisted we swap numbers. I didn't give myself away and I'm open to doing it again sometime very soon. New experience number 34.

Our arms have been linked on the walk back and once we open the front door Ash detaches himself from me and makes his way to the kitchen. I throw myself down on the settee.

"So, did you enjoy yourself?" Ash asks from the other side of the divide.

"It wasn't completely horrible," I admit on a small smile.

He walks into the living room but remains standing, holding a beer in his hand.

"Really?" He laughs "Progress. Seemed like you and Trina hit it off?"

"How could we not? Ignoring her was not an option." I giggle

"Yeah, she's pretty headstrong, but if she hadn't taken a liking to you she wouldn't have acted otherwise. Trina doesn't do fake."

"How long have you known her?"

"We grew up together. After my parents uprooted us to live in Ireland when I was about 7 we moved in next door to Tree and her parents and they became friends so a lot of the time we were thrown together to hang out while our parents mingled."

"You weren't born here?" I'm shocked, this is something else I didn't know about him.

"No, London was our home up until then." *London.* I want to ask what area, push for more but it's pointless. I may have lived there my whole life but I hardly know it. If my parents had been normal, who knows, maybe we'd have gone to the same school and met years ago. Maybe we'd have hated one another.

"Have you and her ever...?" My voice trails off as my cheeks flame.

"Ever what, Fliss?" He smirks

I remain silent so he continues "There's a lot we've done. Have I ever held her hair back while she's thrown up everywhere? Yes. Has she ever slept here? Yes, the spare room might as well have been hers for all the times she's stayed. Has she forced me to play hairdressers and makeup artists? God yes. Stop me if I'm on the wrong track..."

"Have you ever been more than friends?"

"Best friends!" He corrects "And no, that's gross. Plus, I'm not her type."

I scoff before collecting myself. "I'm pretty sure you're most women's type." I blurt and my cheeks burn again. Damn alcohol must have made me loose-lipped.

He doesn't grin though which I've become accustomed to when he receives any kind of compliment. He stares. Hard. As though he's looking right through me. It makes me fidget uneasily. Uncertainty flows through me.

"Am I *your* type, Fliss?" He grins and I'm almost relieved playful Ash is back until I register the question and feel his eyes bore into me. He's not playing.

This is it. Tell the truth, or lie and maybe miss my chance.

End this farce here and now or keep pushing for the dream.

Play it down my head screams. The air is thick with anticipation. My heart pounding at the seriousness in his stare. He's unflinching, waiting just as hard to hear my answer as I am to tell it.

"You're okay." I smile

His face falls but he covers it quickly. Seeing it makes me want to beat myself to a pulp.

He nods as though expecting rejection and turns to leave. I grab his wrist on instinct and he turns my way, uncertainty filling his features, sad eyes seeking mine. "You're not okay Ash. You're everything. You're the best person I know." I admit quietly.

His lips crash to mine in seconds, warm and inviting. Softly at first as though testing he's made the right move but when I respond, when he knows I want this as much as he does, he doesn't hold back. My eyes fall closed. He sinks to the settee never breaking our locked lips, the beer he was holding drops to the floor as he pulls me onto his lap. *I'm straddling Ash.* I can feel how turned on he is and knowing I'm the cause of his lust makes me kiss him eagerly. I've dreamt about this so many times but nothing compares to the real thing.

His hand bunches in my hair, my hands find his face. His kiss is hungry, lethal, *demanding* and it makes me giddy. Our tongues are almost fighting for dominance as they stroke against the other. His hands travel to my arse, pulling me into him, pushing me down onto him.

Panting heavily he pulls back and stares into my eyes. "How much have you drunk, Felicity?"

"What?" I ask exasperated that he's stopped

"I don't want to take advantage..."

"My God, Ash. I'm offering it up. Just take it." I press my lips against him again and he resists for only a second before he's tugging at my dress. Realising it won't budge in our current positions, he picks me up and starts walking. I hear his door slam behind us before he lowers me to his bed. He stands back and stares as he slowly removes his top. I command my body not to squirm, to watch the breathtaking display before me but he's too far away so I sit up and pull him towards me by his belt. He leans forward capturing my lips again and reaching behind me to undo my zipper.

"I like this look on you, Fliss." He murmurs against my lips "Much easier to remove than one of your onesies."

I grin against him. My skin jumps when he touches me again. I don't know why people are so afraid of electrocution, it feels quite nice if you ask me, like a little shot of adrenaline warming my insides.

"I watched you tonight, Fliss. My eyes were on you all night, even when you thought they weren't. You have no idea the effect you have do you?"

When I lean back to stare at him in question he grins and

bends to kiss my neck, inhaling my scent as he does "You're beautiful, Fliss. Inside and out"

Those words, words I've always wanted to hear have an adverse effect. My eyes fill with tears, in a matter of seconds from being all in it's like cold water has been thrown on me, dulling the sensation as my senses kick in and regardless of how much I want this I know I can't have it. Not while I'm still lying to him. When we're together for the first time I want it to be because he really knows who I am, and not by being tricked. He's only skimmed the surface of who I am. My insides aren't beautiful, they're ugly.

He backs up straight away and his eyes burn a hole in my face.

"I'm sorry. I can't. I want to, I just..."

He sits next to me on the end of his bed and runs his hands through his hair sighing heavily as he does so. "You're right."

"I am?"

"Yeah, as much as it pains me to say. We live together, I don't want things to become awkward between us, Fliss. I don't want to lose you and who knows how we'd feel in the morning."

My heart plummets. I might have put a stop to proceedings but I didn't think he'd cave so quickly. He was all over me minutes ago, I thought he'd give me reasons why this would be a good idea. I think there may be something seriously wrong with me and honestly, I never knew I had this much will power. One of my fantasies was about to become true and I turned it down. What happened to living? To grasping all opportunities? *New experiences.*

"I'd better go," I suggest

"Oh no you don't. I don't want any weirdness to have time to develop between us. I'm going to have a cold shower. Stay here, make yourself comfy and we can Netflix and chill."

My eyebrows shoot up "I mean actually chill, Fliss, you know relax?" He laughs but it's a hollow sound.

The following day my head hurts, my brain is mush and my heart aches a little. I fled from Ash's room the second he hit the shower, before we could Netflix and chill. I wasn't sure I wouldn't pounce on the guy. I drag myself from my room reluctantly, praying I didn't go wandering last night and decide it's time to face the music.

Ash is already up, regular as clockwork doing his morning exercise. Usually, I love this, the only acceptable time I can be a pervert. His bare torso slick with sweat, abs on full display as he works out. I usually stand in the kitchen and watch as I eat or drink so no unwanted sounds can escape my lips. It's the high-light of my day. He barely glances my way as I pass through the living room and make my way to the kitchen. Coffee, I need copious amounts of it right now.

I stir slowly, the clanging of the spoon like cymbals in my head and surreptitiously peek at him through the divider. He seems engrossed in press-ups and for once he hasn't asked me to work out with him. Finally, he stops, grabs a towel from the settee, wiping himself down, chugging a bottle of water, then he sits and fires up his laptop, furiously tapping away at the keys. I dread to think what he's writing in his new book if I'm now his muse.

After a few sips of the liquid gold I quietly make my way to the settee and sit across from him, he still doesn't look up. He's purposely ignoring me and being given the cold shoulder by him isn't something I've experienced yet.

I thought I'd become accustomed to silence. Rambling around our big old house alone day in and day out. Turns out though that I've never been privy to awkward silence and that's a whole other ball game.

"Ash?"

He looks up fleetingly before returning his attention to the screen in front of him. "Yeah?" he answers in a tone that screams *go away*.

"Can we talk?"

He sighs and closes his laptop none too gently, placing it next to him before nodding.

I wring my hands nervously in my lap. I don't know what to say. I hate this awkwardness. I want the playfulness back. A tight knot forms in my gut. How do I broach us being *us* again?

"Look, Fliss, if this is about last night we'd both had a bit to drink, inhibitions were lowered and we nearly crossed a line. But we didn't. You don't need to feel awkward. We're good okay? It won't happen again."

If his words were aimed to make me feel better, they don't. His delivery is all off, monotone, matter of fact. None of his usual character behind them so they come out flat and worthless.

I feel my face drop as he says it will never happen again and try to cover it quickly with a small smile as I nod my agreement. "As long as we're on the same page," I say

"The message was loud and clear, Fliss. Don't worry." He says and collects his laptop and walks away. I hear his door close and I feel small. More insignificant than I've felt in a while. What did his last sentence mean? *What message?*

Then it hits me like I've actually been smacked in the face. I stopped what was about to happen. For someone with an ego as big as his bruising it must've stung like a bitch. Does he feel rejected? Unwanted? Or am I just reading too much into it as usual. Maybe for once, I should take his words and their meaning at face value.

I disappear back to my room, get dressed in normal clothes instead of a onesie selection and lie on my bed with my laptop. I hate this emotional distance so decide if I can't speak to him in person, online me can.

Me: Hey, do you have anything for me to look over yet?

Ash: I do, but it's a bit different from my last work. Are you sure you're ready for it?

Me: I'm always ready.

Ash: That's my line! I'll email it over later, some stuff to sort out first.

Me: Are you okay? You sound... Meh.

**Ash: Meh describes it perfectly. I'm good, just a little...
confused I guess.**

Me: Anything I can help with?

**Ash: Maybe. I think I'll just internalise for a bit until I have it
settled in my own mind.**

An incessant tapping pulls me away from our chat exchange.
I wait to see if Ash is going to answer but when the tapping
continues and he doesn't surface, I drag myself from my bed and
go to the front door.

Trina, Jake and Nathan are stood the other side. I almost don't
answer but I need something to distract me, so I paste on a smile
and let them in.

The guys make a beeline for the settee as Trina and I walk to
the adjoining kitchen. I busy myself making tea and coffee as she
chatters non stop about last night. I see Ash walk into the living
room and I'm frozen in his gaze. I turn away so I don't have to
witness the multitude of emotions contained in them.

We join them shortly after and the three of them laugh and
joke as Ash and I offer up the odd nod or smile.

"They need a nickname. You know like Brangelina."
Nathan says

"Who needs a nickname?" I ask, trying to join in and stop
being so unsociable.

"You and Ash apparently." Trina replies rolling her eyes

"I've got it." Nathan says clicking his fingers "Flash!"

I laugh half-heartedly "Or Ass" he offers

"You are not calling us Ass. Why do we need a nickname anyway?"

"Saves time. Instead of asking if Fliss and Ash can come out to play, we can say, oi Flash let's go out."

"That makes no sense you idiot," Jake says

They carry on throwing around power names for us but it doesn't go unnoticed by me how quiet Ash is and apparently not by Trina either as I notice her head ping pong between us both and frowning as she does so.

"Ash, can I talk to you a minute. The function our parents are throwing is giving me acne." She nods towards the kitchen and he follows her with a noticeable stoop to those usually broad shoulders.

His back is facing me but Trina's animated face is clearly visible. I try and squint, to hone in and practice my lip-reading skills but she's going ten to a dozen and Nathan keeps asking my opinion on nicknames.

"How about Fish?"

I shake my head and look back to the kitchen to see they're making their way back to us.

Trina is clearly intuitive as she quickly and efficiently makes the guys leave by physically ushering them out. We arrange a date with one another for the following day and then she sees herself out.

Ash retreats to his room and it's then that I realise he didn't leave me a shower mirror smiley today. *Shit.* I'm really in his bad books.

Chapter 8

Ashton

Trina is many things and when she's on top form like she appears to be today, receiving a lecture from her equates to being stung by a wasp. She told me in no uncertain terms to get off my high horse, quit being a dick and 'suck it up, buttercup.' After laughing at me first, of course.

Being the gem that she is and the person who knows me best in this world taking her advice is the only sensible thing to do, not that I'd ever admit that to her. I wish she'd take her own advice as well, though. She's put me straight.

If I don't want to scare Fliss off then coming on to her last night, being rejected and moody about it this morning and ignoring her is hardly the way to handle it. Being emotionally confused is a new one on me. Turns out the way I handle it isn't very well. This all could have been avoided if she'd waited last night, but she took off and let the void open, let the awkwardness seep in. I finished my shower ready to alleviate any concerns she may have had to find her missing, like she couldn't get away fast enough. That is the crux of my problem. That is what caused my shitty mood because it left time for the rejection and missed opportunity to fester.

A few weeks ago my charm offensive was for selfish reasons but the longer she's here the more natural it becomes. I go out of my way to bring a smile to her face because in turn, it makes me happy. Right now I'm being a jerk which isn't fostering smiles from the one it's easiest to accomplish them with. I'm not one for apologising unless I've seriously fucked up so decide to use my natural charm to get us back on speaking terms without saying that five-letter word.

I walk into the living room and she looks up from where she's writing in that damn journal again.

"Okay, so we're clearly attracted to one another. Something is going to happen between us."

Her eyes widen at my sudden announcement before a hint of a smile plays over her lips. While I have her hooked I continue, "It's inevitable. I'm irresistible, you're irresistible. We're just too tempting. It would be a sin to ignore."

"Oh my God, Ash." She laughs, accompanied by that blush. "You have such a way with words."

The sound and sight of both perk me up immediately so I continue to tease her,

"You know, Fliss, I'm starting to think your sleepwalking is a ploy to tempt me."

"Really?" she questions, playing along.

"How many times are you going to wander into my room naked before my resolve slips?"

"A ploy." She giggles "You think I mortify myself on purpose?

Ash, if I wanted to test your resolve I'd do it while we're both awake."

My eyebrows lift in shock. *Bring it on Fliss.* "Like now?" I grin, only half serious.

"What? No." And I have her back to being flustered. Result.

"Fine, your loss... for now. I'll check again with you tomorrow." I wink at her and leave as quickly as I appeared knowing she'll go back to frantically writing in her journal.

And just like that, we're good again.

Felicity

Current mood – Anxious
Regret level – Yo-yoing

Hanging out with your obsessions best friend is nerve-wracking. Trina is a cool chick and I can see why he's drawn to her. She's confident, likeable and doesn't sugar coat but she's also loyal. I want her to like me because having the best friend on your side is a plus. I also know she's a firecracker and because of her loyalty to Ash, she scares me. Trina is a threat in the most basic of meanings. She won't kill me when she finds out how I've deceived him. No, she'll do something much more inventive.

Trina arrives bright and early. I guess she's one of those weird happy morning people, but then she probably gets quality sleep every night.

She adopts Ash's tactic of looking me up and down when I

answer the door. If she thinks my plain black onesie is a problem I wonder how she'd react to my animal selection of them.

We walk in relative silence for the first few minutes which seems uncanny for Trina. I'm not sure in the short space of time I've known her she's ever been quiet.

We walk until we reach a park and decide to sit on the bench just outside of it.

"I know." She says out of the blue.

I turn to her quickly, panic setting in. Maybe she's dug into me, did research. "Know what?" I ask cautiously

"What happened between you and Ash. I mean, I knew something had gone down by how quiet and uninvolved you guys were but he confirmed it for me."

"Wow, you're sneaky. So there was no function you needed to talk to him about. It was me?"

"Correct."

"Bet that was a fun-filled chat?"

"Depends. It was fun for me to see him miserable over a woman; proves he's human. Not sure if that makes me a sadist enjoying someone else's misery but it did make me happy."

I frown at her as that sinks in.

"You have to understand us four are pretty tight and boy do we love to gossip so when someone new comes into the mix they're gonna be under all kinds of friendly scrutiny. We talk. Jake told me he spoke with you at the bar and what you said about your roommate – he thinks you were joking but I think there was an air of truth in that little confession. Based on what Ash just told me, I don't understand what the problem is?"

"What do you mean?"

"Jeez, this is like high school all over again. Do you like him?" she stares me straight in the eyes and I can't look away.

"Yes," I answer honestly for the first time.

"Right, good. And he likes you."

"He does?"

She throws her hands in the air "How are you guys so blind? I swear just being around you both is nauseating and worrying because I don't know if I'm likely to catch on fire from the heat you're letting off. How can you both not see the blatantly obvious?"

"He likes me?" I smile as it settles in. He isn't just being his naturally flirty self. *Ash likes me.*

"God, Fliss, yes. Why do you think he was up there sulking? Because he likes you but thinks you don't like him. And you're down here liking him but thinking he doesn't like you. Ugh. So now you know. I've put you both straight, so grow up. Stop tiptoeing around whatever the problem is and be adults. I did not sign up to be agony aunt, relationship counsellor or mediator so figure your shit out and I said the same to him so don't think I'm just picking on you."

I start to cry without meaning to. Tears of frustration, genuine sorrow, and relief. I hate that I'm showing weakness to one of the most important women in Ash's life. I would've thought by now that my tear ducts were dried up. I guess not. I've just had the confirmation I've yearned for and I feel sick to my stomach, because it's not *me* he likes, it's the version of me he knows. The one I've presented to him.

"Shit, tough love works on him, but now I know it doesn't on you." She wraps her arms around me and I sob into her hug.

"I'm a terrible person, Tree."

She holds me at arm's length, her brow furrowing, "You kill someone?"

I shake my head "No"

"You planning on killing someone?"

I smile this time "No"

"You kick puppies?"

"No," I grin

"Then nah I don't think you are." She says "And I'm an amazing judge of character."

"I am and I'm in so deep I don't know what to do. We spoke last night... kind of. We're back to being normal with one another – I even had my shower smiley this morning."

"What the hell is a shower smiley?"

I open my mouth to answer and she holds her hand up "Actually, I don't want to know. The visions my mind is conjuring up are much more fun. I still don't understand the problem here though?"

"I just can't go there Tree. I can't tell you why because he needs to hear it first, but I'm nowhere near ready to tell him."

"Wanna talk about it? I think I just proved how amazing I am with the advice." She bumps my shoulder with hers.

"I can't. I can't say the words out loud, just believe me when I say I'm an awful human being and as much as I'd love to pursue something with him I've realised it was all a pipe dream."

"Girl you talk in riddles. Listen, life is simple – we overcomplicate it. And I'm more than qualified to make that statement. If you want something go for it. If there are reasons why you can't, fix them first then go for it. If you're an awful human being, then stop being awful."

"How I would love to be you for a day. You make everything sound so black and white."

"See, Fliss that's exactly where you're going wrong. Nothing is black and white. I live life for the colour in it. Every shade in between the ones you just mentioned make life beautiful and that is simplicity. When we forget that, that's when things go awry. You're so mysterious and I don't think it's necessarily intentional on your part, try to open up, whatever is holding you back I guarantee will be a weight off your shoulders when you do."

Chapter 9

Ashton

I wait for her to return from her walk with Trina. We need to do something fun, shake any lingering funkiness. I wonder if she'd be up for another cooking lesson but then realise we'd likely demolish the kitchen again, as fun as it was, the clean up after was not. I hear her bedroom door close and wait a beat before crossing the hallway towards it. I raise my hand to knock but am stopped by the sound of her hushed voice coming from inside. Curiosity gets the better of me and I find myself leaning against the door to try and listen to her private conversation. Why wouldn't I? I know next to nothing about her and my constant need to know her better is consuming.

"Gerry, I can't come back, not yet."

"I just can't."

"How bad?"

"Okay, but only because it's you asking. I'll get the next flight."

"I'll be home soon. Yes, I've missed you too actually."

I jerk away from the door. My jaw feels like it's set in stone. *Who the fuck is Gerry?* Did she lie about having a boyfriend? What is her deal?

I ready myself to abandon spending time with her and slink off to my room but then it hits me – she's leaving. Catching the next flight. Is that it? She's going back to some other guy? Is that why she stopped last night? She lied about being taken. She couldn't give herself to me because she already belongs to another? This pisses me off. I'm still trying to wrap my head around these sudden feelings and I'm not ready for her to leave. Not ready to watch her walk away before I've had my chance to ... what? What is it I want from her? If I don't know, how the hell can I expect her to be open to it?

My apartment has felt alive again. I love living with her. I never wanted someone in my space, someone I'd have to spend a certain amount of time with. Someone knowing the ins and outs of my routine. Living with someone whether romantically or not is still a huge commitment. And I've just realised I'm all kinds of committed to Fliss. My father has been off my back and I've been happy. I'm not ready to lose any of that. Truth be told, I just don't want to lose *her. But how do I make her stay?* How can I discover if what I want is reflected back?

Felicity

Current mood - Seething, hurt, pissed off (all of the above)
Regret level – Off the charts

This is becoming a habit. Not only do I lie to Ash on a daily, I lie to myself, and now to Gerry. I hung up the phone with no intention of looking for flights. Especially now the time is getting closer and I'm petrified of facing it. I wanted to just hide away with Ash and pretend nothing could hurt me. Pretence is so much more appealing than reality.

Only it seems he had other ideas. He's done a complete one eighty. My escape has become nothing more than another thing to get over.

Tonight, again, I lie here listening to him 'entertaining' the second woman in a row this week. I can honestly say it's like experiencing a new kind of torture. One designed for maximum impact against me. I'm at the end of my tether. After his playfulness a few days ago I thought we were back on track, he seemed to be his normal, easy going, joking self. But that night he was distant. He went out, came home early hours of the morning and he wasn't alone. Jealousy eats me up, anger consumes me and sadness mocks me.

To accompany the laughing, and various other noises coming from the opposite bedroom my mind has decided to conjure up what is actually happening in there. I know, obviously but my mind keeps swaying into great detail, imagining his naked body writhing with a faceless female and in my head, she's butt ugly. Because for some twisted reason that is more acceptable to me. I tell myself he's lowered his standards and is only with them because he can't have me. Not that I believe I'm a catch, but this is my fantasy land and I can make believe whatever I like. To be fair I haven't heard any panting, screaming or yelling of his name but still, it's not rocket science is it? The high pitched giggling and unavoidable flirting is enough to make me gag.

I'm not sure if this is my punishment for getting too close, if he's trying to prove a point or if it's as simple as karma for my deception. All I do know as I lay with a pillow over my head is – I can't take much more. I wish that knowing he was such a man whore made me wise up and get over these silly feelings. But I'm not wired that way. Living with him has only intensified what I already felt. I could leave but my head has clearly decided I like the torture and this is the lesser of two evils. *How messed up is that?*

I turn over and pray to all the gods in the universe that if I fall asleep I will not sleepwalk tonight. The last thing I want to find out in the morning is that I walked in and interrupted them whilst they were at it, or heaven forbid, tried to join in or something equally as mortifying.

The following morning I wait in the hopes that by the time I venture out there his stupid, slutty visitor has left, and also, they didn't receive a visit from me in the dark. I walk out into the living room, bypassing him sprawled on the settee, and make my way to the adjoining kitchen to start on my energy for the day – coffee. The open plan design means we can see each other and I notice him flicking looks my way the same as I send his way. Yet neither of us talk. There's an uneasiness that's been present and I'm desperate for us to get back to how we were. Enough is enough though. We can't spend all day side-eyeing the hell out of one another.

My muscles feel tightly bunched, too much tension for this time in the morning, especially before my morning coffee. I take a sip as I contemplate how to start. How does one broach such a subject?

"Ash?"

"Mmhmm" he answers without so much as glancing my way

"Can we talk?" *I sound like a broken record.*

He puts his phone away albeit reluctantly and stares at me. If I'm reading him right and I think I am because his scowl is unmistakeable then he's annoyed and my own anger flares. What does he have to be annoyed about?

"About what?" he asks and I swear I detect a challenge in his voice, as though he's ready for an argument and I'm walking right into a trap.

"Your, uh... visitors."

He raises his brows and folds his arms, nodding for me to continue.

"Can we maybe limit how many times you entertain in a week? I haven't slept in days." There, that wasn't an unreasonable request. We both live here, there should be give and take between us. I relax now I've said it until I see a slight smirk from him and I'm on guard again.

"You don't sleep anyway, Fliss. Is that really the problem?" He leans forward, arms braced on his legs.

"Regardless of my sleeping habits, it isn't too much to ask for you to have some common decency and take on board what I'm saying."

"Oh, I've taken it on board, I'm just struggling to see why it's an issue."

"If I was bringing a different guy back every night and disrupting your sleep with our ... antics, how would you feel?"

"Why would I give a fuck? I'd think 'good on you' In fact, I'd probably get off listening to it."

"Wow! You're in full jerk mode today."

He jumps up so quickly and strides towards me that I have to grab the counter to keep me steady, and then he's before me, staring into my eyes, while I beg my heart to quieten down. His chest rises and falls in rhythm with mine. He's so near I can feel his body heat and see a vein in his neck pulsing. He clearly has no personal space issues. And then his breath blows over me "If you spoke the truth, Fliss, there isn't anything I'd deny you – within reason, of course. But until you can admit the real problem here, I'll do what I like."

I'm stunned into silence for a moment. *Spoke the truth. Does he know?* I push against his chest to show some kind of reaction and because I really do need him to back up. When he's this close, this intense I can hardly breathe. He barely budges and smirks at my pitiful attempt to remove him from my space. My hand itches to slap him.

"Why are you being like this?" I ask

"This is how I am, Fliss. How I was before you came along. I gave you a settling in period, but I'd say you've firmly got your feet under the table now so normal service can resume. If you don't like it..." He trails off on a shrug, the meaning in that sentence hard to miss. If I don't like it, I can leave.

I should. For my sanity. To spare any further hurt. But I know this isn't him. Do you know how open you can be with someone online, hiding behind a screen, knowing you'll never meet them? How you can rant to them and tell them your innermost thoughts? Well, we did that. Six months of daily conversation clues you in to a person even if it isn't face to face. So, while we've only been physically present together for a few weeks, I know him. His behaviour might be on point but the way he just spoke to me is out of character.

"I'll pack then," I say as a test

His eye twitches, to most it would be indiscernible. But I've studied him these last few weeks, it's a tell of his. And that was nothing more than an idle threat. I can't figure out why but he's pushing my buttons, testing me and trying to push me away. Maybe if I wasn't so full of lust, so devoid of anything else meaningful in my life I'd take the hint and leave. But I don't feel like our story is over yet. We're barely past the first few chapters and if a conflict is what he wants then I'm all for being the antagonist.

When he doesn't respond I continue, "Okay, I will." I retort as I make my way past him. He grabs my arm and pulls me back so I bump up against the countertop. He presses into me, an arm around my waist and despite myself, I succumb to his touch. I want him to always look at me with this kind of drunken lust. "Ready to test that resolve?" he murmurs

He tips his head as I tilt mine and our lips collide. All of our pent up frustrations are released in this one breathtaking display. We're greedy, devouring one another, breathing heavily, touching frantically.

The background noise I hardly paid attention to suddenly stops and I realise it's the sound of the shower being turned off. I spring back from him, watching as his head falls and he mutters "Fuck." A few seconds later the door opens and I cut my gaze back to Ash. He has the decency to take a step back from me and look ashamed.

In walks the girl from my first visit, the same girl I stole the room from, wearing nothing but a towel, long blonde hair dripping all over my floor. Alarm bells start ringing in my head.

She's concentrating so hard on perfecting her flirtatious walk, staring down at her legs that she doesn't notice me as she addresses Ash "Maybe we should try that again?" she purrs before her head lifts.

I want to hurl and throw daggers at Ash. My hand flies to our rules list pinned to the fridge beside me, my finger tapping it as my gaze conveys every emotion I'm concealing. *No wandering naked women.*

"Oh, it's you," Barbie says noticing my presence for the first time. She looks me up and down as seems customary for everyone recently. Her brow furrows in utter disdain. She snaps her head from me to Ash, looking repeatedly between us. Then out of the blue, she points my way and explodes, "*That!* You prefer that to this?" she screeches as runs her eyes over herself.

"You're kidding me right?" she shakes her head and before I can retort she continues, "I thought we were making headway, is *she* really the reason you haven't touched me yet?"

She starts pacing and both myself and Ash watch, he seems amused by her dramatic show whilst I'm biting my tongue, just biding my time as my anger grows.

"You're losing it, Ash, lowering your standards. Look at what she's wearing for fuck sake, what woman in their right mind dresses like that? She'll never measure up to me."

His amused grin slips as he jumps to my defense "She's already exceeded you, Cammy. She isn't a spiteful bitch who thinks walking around flaunting her flesh is what I want."

Both of them talking about me as if I'm not stood right fucking there has me ready to blow.

Hurt flitters across her features before a mask slips back in place " So you want someone who dresses up as an animal – a pig no less? You used to love my flesh, Ash. Don't pretend otherwise."

"I loved the idea of you but that was before I knew you, before I found out how ugly your soul is."

"You're just saying that for her benefit." She looks at me in complete confusion "You want me, you clearly need someone who knows how to be feminine why else would you have brought me here the last few nights?"

"For a much-needed reality check, nothing more. You served your purpose now get dressed and leave."

"Seriously? This isn't over Ash. Do you think you can just dismiss me? You think you can lead me on and then discard me?" She laughs humourlessly "Think again." She turns to walk away and lets the towel drop to the floor, showing her tanned and tone backside. "Pretend you don't want this all you like but I can feel your eyes all over me." She throws over her shoulder.

As soon as she's stashed away in his room I move to leave.

"Fli-"

"Don't." I spin around to face him anger seeping from every pore. How dare he. "You used her to make me jealous? You brought her here intentionally to get under my skin, to hurt me. I had you all wrong Ash. I never pegged you for being a game player. I guess you're pettier than I realised. You disgust me," I explode

"I never touched her," He says meekly

"So? You made me believe you did, made me endure sitting in my room listening to her laughing and flirting, making me imagine..."

He strides forward, boxing me in by placing his arms either side of me on the counter "What?" He demands

I shake my head "It doesn't matter."

"Yes it does. Why won't you just say it? Just admit you feel this too."

I stare at him, tears brimming again "I did. Now I'm not so sure. That move was uncalled for. The next move is mine."

I push past him but he grabs my forearm stopping me "I'm all for playing games if it'll result in winning, don't think for a second I'll give up making you confront what's between us however I have to."

"What is between us Ash, apart from a whole load of deception?"

"Don't act like you're the only wronged party here. Who's Gerry?"

My eyes widen, wondering how he even knows that name. "He works for me."

It's then it dawns on me why he did this. He was jealous, felt threatened, envisioned Gerry was *my boyfriend?* Lover? It's laughable.

"This was tit for tat? Next time don't eavesdrop and if you want to know something, ask."

"I do, you don't divulge anything."

I yank my arm free. "Tu non capisci Sei tutto ciò che voglio, non posso proprio averti." And I leave him standing there. I don't want to be around when barbie Cammy reappears.

"I'll look that up, Fliss. Stop hiding behind other languages and tell me how you really feel." He shouts after me.

I close my door and climb into bed. How did we get here? We

were best friends. We respected and appreciated one another. Now, because I forced something through a lie we're arguing, one-upping each other. He's offering what I came here for I should be grabbing it with both hands. It was my sole purpose. But distance away from my home circumstances has cleared my head too much. The escape and reprieve has been great for me. I've shed some insecurities. I've taken what I needed, I've grown up and I'm stronger. Strong enough to go back, to face it.

Ash is not only believing the lie, he's wanting it.

Would he still want me if he knew the truth?

Chapter 10

Ashton

Fliss retreated to her room, thinking she can hide away, but she'll have to resurface at some point and we will have to fix this. Cammy stormed out and I'm sat trying to write my story which includes too much of my own life. I know they say to write what you know but this is too personal even for me. I've written insta- love. I never thought it was an actual thing though. And by love, I don't really mean love. I don't love her, but she creates some pretty intense feelings in me and that's more or less the same thing. For knowing someone a couple of weeks its unnerving. But she's become pretty much all I think about. What pisses me off more is I don't really know her. I know nothing substantial about her at all. Sure, I know how to make her blush, how to make her smile. I know her love for onesies. I sense her innocence. But apart from that... *nothing, nada*. She just appeared one day and slotted into my life effortlessly.

She doesn't talk about her family, friends, why she moved away from them. She says she has a job, but I've never seen her answer calls or do any actual work. I don't know how she affords to pay me rent when she barely leaves the apartment. She's an enigma. One who's managed to get under my skin without trying the normal tactics women use and maybe that's the draw. The mysteriousness. She's funny, sweet, quirky as fuck and doesn't act like she's trying to hook me, yet she's hooked me anyway. Is it a simple case of reverse psychology? Is it the romance I'm currently writing trying to imprint on me?

I know she's feeling this too, we're constantly skirting around one another. I see the way she looks at me, it's the same as I look at her, like she wants to revolve around me. *So why the holding back?* Keeping me at arms length. You don't kiss someone the way she just did if you aren't in to them. It can't just be because we live together, because even though I vowed I wouldn't fuck around with my flatmate it didn't take long to change my mind. More importantly, I don't want to mess around, I don't want a fling or even a friends with benefits situation. *I want exclusivity.*

I know in my gut there's something more going on here and I'll push until she spills. Persistence is one of my better traits. My tactic to do so may have been wrong, questionable even but at least it unearthed something, she opened up, gave me a clue. I'm sick and tired of pussyfooting around. It ignited the fire in her and I need to keep on while it's simmering.

I walk towards her room determined to apologise. I hope she isn't one for asking what I'm apologising for because as a man I really have no idea. I just know I'm in the wrong on so many levels. I guess the way I spoke to her this morning was out of order but she's so goddamn frustrating. Flaunting Cammy was another huge no-no. It worked but god knows what I was thinking. I can't stand the woman, we've never been a couple, but yeah I've fucked her. She was hard to shake, even managing to find out when I had flat viewings and turning up at the same time as them, turning them away with her catty attitude, acting like the nightmare girlfriend that no one in their right mind would choose to be around. I only brought her back because she was easy pickings and would never turn down an offer from me. Perfect for what I wanted to achieve which was bringing out the green-eyed monster in the girl I'm actually interested in.

I've been wondering why Fliss is still here, after telling *Gerry* she was booking a flight. Even pushed her to leave knowing she told some other guy she would. Why would she stay and put up with my behaviour that clearly has left a bad taste in her mouth when she has somewhere else to be? Someone else to be with. Could it be because she's also feeling this undeniable pull or is she here because she's escaping from someone? *Is being here with me nothing more than a diversion?* She admitted I made her jealous, that means she feels and that's something I can work with. If she's jealous, she wants this too.

I hear her whisper hissing and can't resist the temptation to listen in again. I've never been so damn nosey my whole life but twice in the space of days she has me wishing I had a glass handy to press up against her door. She's so tight lipped, I know next to nothing about her and if eavesdropping can give me an insight then why not?

"I am. I promise this time."

"Okay, it's not easy for me, you know?"

"By the end of the week, I'll be home."

I get an awful sinking feeling in my stomach. Well, that's *not* happening. If I have to thrust the paperwork she signed in her face then damn straight I will. Not only because I don't want her to go but because I need her to stay. For my sanity. And I can't afford for her to leave, I'll be up shit creek and my father's gloating is not something I want to witness.

The door opens and I'm caught red-handed as I steady myself from falling forward. Her hands fly to her hips, her nose scrunches and even now when everything is up in the air, the sight of it is amusing. Fliss can't pull off angry, especially since she's changed out of the bright pink pig onesie, curly tail and all to wear a more ferocious animal design.

"Hear anything good?" she demands

"I thought I heard vibrating, was just coming to check on you." I grin

Her eyes narrow, "That's funny, I had the setting on low, you know to maintain my *privacy.*" She retorts

That's more like it. Spar with me, Fliss.

"I have the hearing of an elephant Fliss, no hiding anything from me."

"It's the memory of an elephant, Ashton."

"What animal hears well, then?"

She rubs her temples "Can I help you with something? I'm not in the mood for *this Ash* right now, can't you try being a dick again, it would make this a lot easier?"

"Ouch."

"Oh, I'm sorry. Did I hurt your feelings? I thought it was a new thing we were trying out, instead of being decent people." Sarcasm drips from every word she speaks.

"Whoa, did I bring out a tough side to you. I think I like it."

She sighs heavily, rubbing circles in her temples "Ash, seriously. I can't do this right now, so, did you need something?"

"Can we move from the doorway?"

"If it's going to make you talk faster, then yes." She glides past me and I don't even know what animal it is she's wearing, where does she find these onesies? She must have them specially made because I can't imagine these things are wholesale. If I had to guess and only because of the long green tail traipsing behind her I'd go for lizard/dinosaur half breed.

I shake my head as I follow her, biting my lip from making a comment on it and being careful not to trip over the tail. How I'm going to keep a straight face and attempt a version of an apology whilst she's sat looking like that I don't know. It's then I notice her bare feet. I'm not a foot guy, but for the first time, I take in the fact that the second toe on her right foot wears a small gold band. A toe ring. And suddenly, *I am* a foot guy, because that is sexy as fuck, even if the rest of her is adorned in a dinosaur costume.

We sit opposite one another as we regularly do. It's strange but we seem to have adopted these seating preferences. I never sit in her seat and she never ventures to mine either unless we're watching a film.

Fuck me. This onesie has a hood which she now pulls over her head, watching for my reaction to the white dinosaur spikes sticking up, silently challenging me to mock it. *Nice move, Fliss.* Spikes and a tail – is she trying to make this harder? I'm determined to not let her throw me off but the sight of her before me dressed like a fucking dinosaur is too much to let slip. I swallow down the laughter desperate to escape and press my lips into a thin line, eager to contain myself.

She raises her eyebrows impatiently, all she's missing is tapping her imaginary watch to let me know I'm on a timescale.

"I'm sorry," I say

"For?" she asks

Dammit, she is one who wants to know the ins and out of my fuck-ups. From the determined way she glares at me, I won't be let off the hook that easily.

"Everything." I try

"Everything?" she scoffs. "That encompasses a lot, *Ashton*. How can I accept your apology unless you narrow it down?" She crosses her arms but I don't miss the sparkle in her eye.

"Speaking to you like shit this morning?"

"That's a question. Are you seriously just guessing? Because an apology isn't an apology if you don't know why you're giving one."

"For eavesdropping?"

She rolls her eyes "We're going to be here all day at this rate."

I sigh and rub my neck "For bringing Cammy here, for hurting you. For being so out of line I don't even recognise myself."

Her eyes narrow but on a resigned sigh, she says, "I accept your questionable apologies. Are we done?"

"No. Stop being so dismissive. What can I do better? I don't want to be responsible for pissing you off. It makes me feel like crap. I'll be more considerate, no more games, at least I'll try, but seeing as I can't even get an apology right I'll likely mess up. Just tell me what I can do tomorrow for a fresh start?"

She stands and starts walking away. My shoulders slump, usually my charisma lets me get away with murder around her. I must've really hurt her. And then she throws me a bone. Just before rounding the corner and without looking back she says "I want my shower smiley."

I silently fist pump. I may not be forgiven but she's thawing. I haven't lost my touch.

Most girls want flowers, jewellery or chocolate. But not Fliss, a simple smiley face on a steamed-up bathroom mirror. Easy to please doesn't even come close to this woman.

Piece of cake.

Felicity

Current mood – Indecisive
Regret level – Through the roof

I haven't even opened my eyes yet but can feel the migraine building before I do. I roll over, trying to get closer to the wall touching the side of my bed, needing the feeling of being enclosed. I meet a wall but not the brick kind. The wall I press up against is warm, heat radiating from it. I open one eye and my hand flies to my mouth. For fuck sake! This is getting beyond a joke now. I'm in Ash's bed again, only it appears this time I didn't disturb his sleep, I just got in next to him. I look down at myself, relieved to find my pyjamas still in place. I scoot away to the other end as quietly as I can. If I can escape before he wakes up then I'm home free, he'll never know and won't have another story to hold over me. I reach the edge and sit up –

"Where are you going?"

Busted.

He rolls over to face me, propping his head up with his arm, torso exposed, ensuring I can't look away.

"Were you hoping I wouldn't notice? Because I've been awake a long time, you know in case you tried to kill me in my sleep."

I fall back against the mattress, cursing as I do.

"Ash, I, you're probably sick of this but again I'm sorry. I don't know why I keep doing it." I don't look at him, my eyes remain on the ceiling.

"Did you do it this much at home?" he asks

I turn to face him, mirroring his position as I rest on my own arm. "No, months could go by without it happening. Maybe it's you, I'm allergic or something."

He laughs "Or maybe you're so attracted to me and suppressing it that at night your subconscious wants to act out all the kinky shit you keep locked away."

I blush, because he may be on to something. He sees it though. "No shit. That's why you're doing it more? Because I'm such a stud? Irresistible?" he's incredulous.

"Well, it wouldn't be because you're modest would it?"

He grins "Just playing to my strengths. You can't touch my brain, but my body..." he opens his arms wide in invitation and flashes those dimples.

I feel myself blush. Torso and dimples at stupid o'clock in the morning? *I'm so screwed.*

"You don't have to go you know. You can sleep in here if you need to be next to me so desperately."

As I contemplate that option he takes that moment of indecision and grabs me, pulling me down and against him until we're spooning. I'm rigid for a moment until I relax into being held by him. It's such a welcome feeling, comforting beyond belief. I've had more affection in the last few weeks than I've had in an entire year. I didn't realise how much I needed it.

I can't close my eyes, though. I'm now wide awake, savouring the fact that his arm is around me, his nose nuzzled into my neck and his body heat surrounding me, I tentatively move my hand bringing it to rest on top of his over my stomach. He makes a contented sound and switches our hands so he can intertwine his fingers in mine.

"Go to sleep, Fliss. Relax, I've got you, you're not going anywhere." He places a gentle kiss below my ear and in minutes I'm out.

At home, time used to take an eternity to pass, but then it started going by too quickly before I had a chance to gather my thoughts, and now it has finally run out completely. And the timing sucks because Ash and I are better than ever. Closer than before and affectionate nonstop. It's my dream come true but I've promised I'll go back home. Gerry is insistent but worse than that he's right. I've had my time. I've already been gone longer than I ever intended. This was supposed to be a lapse, lasting no longer than a week tops and it's already been nearly a month. I took my break but now I have to face the music. I can't keep delaying the inevitable. I can't stall any longer. I've realised I can't leave Ash in this limbo, giving him half of me and also never letting it lead anywhere. It's just as difficult for me. It would be so easy to just give in, tell him everything he wants aligns with what I want. The more time we spend together the more the line blurs. We're essentially a couple yet haven't been physically intimate. So I've reached my conclusion. I don't want this, this way. Nothing could ever really blossom between us when our start is full of lies. It's the ultimate dilemma. Coming clean means this is over but continuing to lie and lead him on when it will come out, in the end, will hurt him more in the long run.

This is a twisted brand of manipulation because there's no malice intended but that will ultimately be the end result.

The saddest part is I've realised life isn't always about being happy, it's about being content. He's given me both which makes me richer than anyone.

I'm making us a meal. And by making I mean, I ordered in burger meal deals. This is meant to be a goodbye meal and while it isn't fancy it sums us up perfectly, not that Ash has any idea this is the last meal we will share together. I'm going to break it to him over dinner. I'm steeling myself to tell him the truth in the hopes that not only will it ease my conscience but that there will be no fighting for me to stay. That'll be the last thing he will want. Two birds, one stone.

I've dressed for the occasion, discarded my onesies in favour of a crimson ladylike dress. It accentuates all my curves and the neckline displays some serious cleavage. I'm going to need every advantage tonight to ease into the anarchy.

"Mmmm, I love the smell of burning." He says, appearing out of thin air and sitting at the candlelit table. We may be having takeout burgers but that doesn't mean I didn't dress the table romantically.

"Nothing is burnt, thank you very much, it's well done." I smile

"Just for the record, I know you ordered in." he grins

"I did not. I slaved over this meal." I wink

"In that case, I take it back. In all seriousness, though I hope you didn't order from the takeaway down the road, they're known to add dog to their meat."

My face drains of colour. *Shit.*

"Gotcha. It's too easy, babe." He smirks

I flush every time he uses that endearment, he started it a few days ago. The first time he called me that, he looked just as shocked as I was but now it's natural for him. "Stop using those against me," I warn

He grins harder and those bloody indentations on his cheeks draw me in "I have no control over them." He shrugs, false innocence written all over his face.

"Oy yes you do, Ashton. You wield them to your advantage every opportunity you get. You know they're my weakness."

"Then we're even."

"Explain," I demand

"You're *my* weakness, especially when you call me Ashton."

And just like that, I melt. How can he change my on edge mood in a nanosecond just by being sweet?

He pulls me into his lap and kisses me, a real smacker, before releasing me and swatting my arse. I yelp as I steady myself before stepping to the seat next to him and lowering myself into it.

"You're perky today."

"Want to know why?" he asks

I shrug

"You left *me* a shower smiley today. Your first one. Though it looked a little deformed, you need to practice your smiley skills."

"It was meant to look deformed."

"Really?"

"Yes, to show that we all have flaws."

He bursts out laughing "Bullshit."

"We can't all be perfect at everything Ash. I'm better at other things."

"Like cooking?" he chuckles

"I might have hidden talents."

"Like naked sleepwalking?"

"I don't really sleepwalk. Never have." I say just as he takes a bite of his burger.

His eyes snap up to meet mine and I try to remain serious.

"You're shitting me?"

"No, honestly. When I came to view this apartment I had no idea my flatmate was going to be so hot so I devised a plan."

He swallows another mouthful and I watch in delight at his cogs turning.

"So that first night I gave up my bed for nothing?"

"Not for nothing. I had an amazing sleep in your double bed, thank you very much. My room is too cold."

"I'll keep you warm and then you wouldn't have to pretend to sleepwalk into my room, you'd already be there."

"Maybe tonight I'll take you up on that offer."

His eyebrows almost shoot through the ceiling. Although this is fun I decide to come clean. I can't lie about everything.

"Chill out Ash. Of course, I sleepwalk. I'd never do the stuff I do just to get your attention, though your belief in it says a lot about your ego."

"If we're telling the truth. Your shower smiley never made me that happy."

I pretend to jab my fork in my heart and twist it around.

He laughs "Okay that was another lie but I am happy about something else... my book is nearly finished, just need to hear from my beta reader."

"That's amazing. Can I read it?"

"Umm, don't take this the wrong way, but I'd prefer you waited until it's perfect. My beta is amazing at pointing out flaws and making suggestions for it to be the best it can. She really should be the first person to lay eyes on it after me."

"Should I be jealous? Your beta sounds pretty important to you?"

"Oh yeah, really jealous, like spitting mad. I love my beta."

"Do they have a name?"

"Yes."

"Well? Is it a secret?"

"Yes, I think I'll protect my beta's identity... for now."

"So mysterious, Ash. Now I'm really worried."

"Okay, but this is a secret, you can't tell anyone. Swear?" he jokes

I raise my palm, mocking making an oath "I swear on the holy flatmate covenant to never tell a soul the real identity of said beta."

He nods, but just to be totally satisfied he holds his pinky out "Pinky swear?"

I roll my eyes but wrap my pinky with his, swearing as I do. "Need me to find a bible to swear on as well?"

"No need. A pinky swear is way more binding than anything else." He tells me.

"Come on then." I urge

"Monty."

"You put me through all that for Monty?" I shake my head as he grins and shovels some fries in his mouth "Okay. Gender?"

"Female, obviously."

"How did you find her?"

"I didn't. She found me. She read my first book and loved it, sent me a pm and we've been screen besties ever since."

"Ha, I win. She can't leave you shower smileys from a screen."

"Yeah, but she can send me some pretty amazing pictures."

I frown, knowing I've never sent him pics until it dawns on me, the one I did send of my lips. I suddenly feel in competition with myself and it's bizarre.

We finish our meal and move to the corner settee to snuggle up for a film.

"Thank you." He says nuzzling my neck

"Don't thank me yet, Ashton. I have one more surprise up my sleeve. Are you ready?"

"I'm always ready, you know that." He winks

I jump up and run to the kitchen, grabbing pre-prepared bowls of sweets for our film night. I hand them to him and a wide smile stretches across his face.

"You took out all the green ones. That's love." He tells me grinning like I've just presented him with the best gift in the world.

"That's preparation." I joke back "Otherwise I have to sit watching you rifle through the packets, fishing them out and it's annoying."

"Love." He argues

"If this equates love to you Ash then you're really easy to love."

I'm vaguely aware of being lifted, moved and placed down on something soft again. A gentle kiss is pressed to my forehead "Sleeping beauty." He murmurs before I hear my door click shut quietly.

I sit bolt upright. Shit, I fell asleep. I had plans for us tonight. Secret farewell plans that didn't involve falling asleep and dribbling on him.

I throw myself back and lie here, staring at the ceiling, kicking myself for not being more alert. The new me can be bold though, right? I've changed, become more confident. Tonight is my last night here, it has to be and I'm wasting it letting my mind tie me up in knots. Across the hall is everything I've ever wanted. I wanted him when he was nothing more than a distraction and a profile picture, since living with him, that want hasn't diminished, but grown. And this is my last chance.

I throw my covers back, tiptoe to my door and on a deep breath decide to take control. I walk into his room, he's awake as I knew he would be, staring at his ceiling too, his exposed torso illuminated by a bedside lamp. He turns my way his eyes lighting up with curiosity and tinged with hope. Not a word passes between us as I discard my dress and stand before him in my best lacy underwear. His tongue swipes across his lips as he waits for my next move.

A shiver of anticipation runs down my back.

"Please tell me you aren't sleepwalking." He groans

I smile and shake my head, biting my lip as I take a step closer. I'm trying to portray confidence I don't possess, because my inexperience could ruin this.

"There'll be no stopping me this time, Fliss." He warns "So be sure before you come any closer."

I take another step towards him, emboldened by the lust and need in his heated stare. "I've never been more sure about anything or anyone, Ash."

The grin I receive is full of sin and delicious promise.

He jumps out of bed and circles me before coming to stand right before me. My breath hitches as he rakes his gaze all over, appreciation reflected in his eyes as he takes in every curve of my body. His hand curls around the nape of my neck, pulling me closer until our lips meet. No hesitation, no caution just blatant need. He kisses me so hard the pain tingling my lips sears through my entire body. I'm turned on from his kiss alone. His hands slide down my back until they meet my arse "You still have too many clothes on, Fliss." He says before claiming my lips again, when he pulls back he challenges "Take them off."

I can feel his impatience, he's itching to remove them himself but he's figuring out what I like, what I'll do and how I'll react. I'm learning right along with him. I'm in his hands and willing to let him mould me however he pleases. He can take control because I may have initiated this but I don't know what the hell I'm doing. I slowly pull down my thong, pulling on knowledge from films I've seen, letting it drop at my feet before stepping out of them. Next, I reach behind me to unhook my bra "Eyes on me, Fliss."

When I look up at him on his command his heated gaze is enough to scald me. I have no problem complying with that request. There's nothing better than looking into his eyes on a normal day, even more so now when I get to see them dilate and watch as the colour darkens.

I let my bra drop to the floor and stand before him naked, for the first time I actually remember being. The urge to wrap my arms around myself is huge. *New experience.* He sucks in a breath before consuming me with his mouth again. Stealing away any self-consciousness or self-doubt. Kissing him, like this, is pure unadulterated bliss.

I tug at his boxers, acting on impulse, wanting to feel his skin on mine and he steps out of them without breaking our kiss. He lifts me by my arse cheeks and my legs automatically wrap around him. I'm placed on a chest of drawers, the coolness of the unit making me gasp. He stands between my legs feathering kisses and nipping at my skin. His tongue swipes across my nipple and I grip onto his shoulders, my fingers digging into his flesh. My eyes close and head falls back riding the sensations, letting him work his magic.

"Eyes on me." He repeats "Keep them on me."

He removes me from the unit muttering "I want you in my bed." He places me on the mattress so delicately as though I'm something precious. His body rests over me, moving lower and lower until his breath reaches the apex of my thighs. He teases my clit with his tongue agonisingly slowly and I jerk at the unfamiliar contact. My back arches off the bed, causing him to chuckle against me before holding me still with one hand splayed over my lower stomach. He resumes his slow torture on me until I'm nothing but a mass of heightened nerves. My hands fly to his hair and I tug at it before pushing his face into me. He growls and becomes relentless in his mission to kill me off. Pressure starts to build and I desperately chase. His mouth clamps completely over me as his tongue swirls unforgivingly.

Faster and faster, he takes me higher, my legs tremble and I feel like my body is nothing but exposed nerves. He's relentless in his teasing until I don't think I can take anymore, I'm on the precipice "Fuck, Ash!" I yell

He continues with even more fervour, my words egging him on, he knows I'm close, can feel my trembling. My hands claw at the mattress as a wave of euphoria takes over my body, climbing and climbing until I'm shouting incoherently, thrashing and moaning my pleasure for the whole building to hear. He works me down before crawling up my body, a satisfied glint to his eyes and grin on his face "You have a dirty mouth, Fliss." He grins wickedly "And fuck, does it turn me on."

He claims my mouth in a heated kiss, making me forget where it's just been, until I taste myself on him. He continues to kiss me senseless as he lines himself up with my entrance. He presses forward aiming to penetrate again and again before freezing as though he's had an epiphany.

"You're a virgin?!"

I bite my lip. Well, this is awkward.

"In about 5 seconds I won't be if you quit stalling." I front it out.

He raises his eyebrows, desire replaced by shock and indecision written all over him "Fliss how, why?"

"I guess I've never found anyone I thought was worth giving myself to like this. So completely." I shrug as if it's no big deal. I don't want this to stop. I don't want him questioning if this is a good idea. I want to feel him inside me. *Need* to.

I raise my hips in invitation, trying to erase the doubt I now see from him "Don't stop." I whisper before placing my lips on his "Give me this, take what you need from me, Ash. Please."

He rests on his elbows as his hands come up to cup my face. He kisses me deeply and it feels a whole lot like gratitude before he surges forward, his dick inside me. He stares into my eyes as my nails dig into his back. My pulse races as the bite of pain soon gives way to pleasure and all the while he doesn't remove his eyes from mine. *Adoration* the only sight I see. We're locked in. There's no more talking, just feeling, complete and utter devotion. Everything I feel in this moment is reciprocated. I can see he's trying to maintain his control, to hold on to it, wanting my first experience to be a great one.

I may not be experienced but I know what I need, pleasuring myself is all I've had, so I lift my fingers and his eyes widen but he doesn't give up his pace. I snake my hand between my legs, playing with myself as he surges in and out.

"Fuck, Fliss!" he groans

My entire being is electrified. A complete sensory awakening. The heat builds again, my head lolls and my eyes flutter closed.

"Eyes on me, Fliss."

I snap them open and the sight of the heat radiating from them with an intensity I never thought would be bestowed upon me has me screaming out, clenching my walls around him, squeezing his dick. He lets out a strangled moan, roaring until we're both spent, coming down from our shared high. He doesn't move for a while, resting his head against my neck. Spent but satisfied. I try to catch my breath, to make sense of the emotions I'm wading through. When he does move it's to pull out gently and roll next to me, pulling me against him, my head to his slick chest. His strong arms wrap around me as I run my fingers over his chest.

"You're something else, Fliss." He breathes before kissing my head and holding me tight. "Are you okay?"

I nod "Better than okay." I reply

A surge of happiness runs through me. I never want to let him go.

"Stay with me, Fliss. Promise me." It's spoken so tenderly I'm nearly reduced to tears.

I don't know if he means stay here in his bed with him for the night or stay with him always. Either way, it isn't something I can vow.

I stand in his doorway watching him as he sleeps, my heart heavy. Seeing him like this, peaceful, content is heart clenching. Something shifted between us last night. I felt it to my soul. An emotional significance that will never be forgotten. I never should have gone to him but don't regret it now for a second. Fate compelled me and last night was the perfect way for this to end. Because I always knew it had to.

He might be hurt, upset even but after what we shared disappearing from his life as fast as I entered it is all I can give him to lessen the blow in the long run. My feelings don't come into the equation. I started this and now I have to end it, regardless of how sick and empty, it makes me feel.

I linger for a moment more before reluctantly walking away. I grab my pre-packed suitcase from my room, take one last look around the place I think of as home and leave as quietly as possible.

Maybe this is how my dream has to end because deception doesn't deserve a reward.

Chapter 11

Felicity

Current mood - Melancholy
Regret level - Infinite

I walk into my house and the familiar silence hits me. I stand in the entryway, the cold, uninviting space laughing at me for even thinking I'd never set foot here again. My little excursion was just a momentary blip. Exhausted after my flight and the many tears I've shed, I discard my case, make a beeline for my room, change into a onesie and crawl into bed. Tomorrow is a big day. One I'm wholly unprepared for. The guilt and shame are back, vying to take first place. Life is so unfair. I ugly cry myself to sleep.

Morning comes around too quickly and I find myself at this place once more, walking through the same corridors, receiving the same pitying looks from the nurses, but this time their looks are tinged with judgement, little shakes of their heads, whispering to one another.

And it's deserved so I keep my head down, avoiding them all instead of lashing out like my tongue itches to.

I reach her room and enter silently, waiting just inside the doorway for a moment to compose myself. I command my feet to walk forward, my steps sluggish and perch myself on the edge of the bed. I can't bring myself to look at her, so I grasp her hand and hold it in mine. She's warm, physically.

"Mum. It's me Felicity."

She turns and stares through me. No recognition visible at all on her aged features. My parents were in their early fifties when they had me so I'm used to my mum being 'old' but looking how she does now is still a shock. In the time I've been gone she seems to have doubled in age appearance wise. My heart sinks just as it does every time. Because whenever I come to visit a tiny part of me always believes that this will be the day she knows me. That some small inconsequential part of the jigsaw and muddled memories will allow her to remember me in some small way – even just my name. But what I really hope for is that she'll remember she's my mum and I'm her daughter instead of the complete and utter stranger she now knows me to be. Ever since her diagnosis, I've thought of her as frozen and I guess she is. When you hear words like dementia and Alzheimers you generally only think about the memory loss but this illness steals so much more than that from you. Thinking, behaviour, attention, concentration, language, and feelings are all affected. It's like the person you once knew died.

And I *left* her.

Dealing with our role reversal, watching her decline was too much to bear. So I ran away. I found my escape and the guilt of that decision sits heavily on my chest. I convinced myself it was okay because she wouldn't notice if I didn't visit, she wouldn't miss me as she has no recollection of me. But that doesn't make it okay. It's not even close to being acceptable. She would have never deserted me while I was going through an illness this disabling. I wasn't ready to be a carer, not for the person whose job it is to care for me. But after my escape, I now realise how immature I was, how wrapped up in cotton wool and unprepared for real adulthood. I wasn't equipped for any of this. I failed her and in a way she failed me.

Our family dynamic has been irreversibly altered and I didn't know how to sift through the range of feelings it invoked. It started with anger which morphed into denial. Her quick decline was so devastating to watch that eventually, all I felt was sadness, despair, and frustration. And the burning desire to flee. To get as far away as possible. To pretend that this wasn't happening – not to my mum. Abandoning all that I knew was a childish coping mechanism. And the worst part is, while I was with Ash I enjoyed myself. I laughed and was happy again. I was living instead of being frozen just like her. I didn't give her a second thought. I abandoned her all so I could concentrate on myself and my needs and wants. This is the first time I'm glad she can't remember me because she'd be ashamed and heartbroken.

I had no friends, no one I could tell my deepest darkest fears to, no one of any consequence I could lean on or cry to on our lowest days. My mum was my best friend. The only friend I needed and losing her even though she's still in the flesh was the hardest thing I've ever faced alone.

And now I'm mad. At myself. At the world. At the complete unfairness.

She doesn't have long left and I wasted all the time I could've spent with her on Ash. I want nothing more than to crawl onto the bed with her, wrap my arms around her and feel her wrap hers around me. I want to hold her. Inhale her scent and commit it to memory. I want to feel her stroke my hair with the tenderness she always did and reassure me everything is going to be okay. At this moment in time, I'd happily accept a lecture from her. I want her to shout at me, tell me off. I need her to show me her fire hasn't been completely extinguished.

But I don't have that luxury. So I stare at her, memorising every line on her face and committing it to my memory as she stares back at me and I pray that my presence alone however confusing is bringing her some peace and reassurance.

A tear slides down my cheek and before I know it all the emotions I've been running from and bottling up come flooding out. My shoulders start to shake from the force of my muffled sobs and I let my head drop to her bed.

I'm not ready to be without her.

I'll always need her.

I cry into her bedsheets like I've never cried before. Our life together playing through my mind and when I think my heart has finally broken I feel a graze on my head. I freeze for a moment before turning my head slightly and see ing my mum still just staring at me but somehow she's managed to muster the strength to move her hand and lay it on my head. No stroking or patting, it's just resting on me and through my tears, I smile, like a rainbow through the rain. Some motherly instinct reached out to me when I needed it the most.

"I love you mum," I whisper

Ashton

Aftermath is an ugly thing. More ugly than the cause of it.

But that's what her leaving caused.

Waking up to find Fliss gone, not only from my bed but from the apartment fucking hurt. At first, I didn't understand, but once it started to sink in, it doesn't take a genius to figure it out. Was I not worth a goodbye? A fucking explanation? Was a conversation too much to expect? But more than hurting it unleashed anger. I've spent the last few days taking out my torment and fury on the apartment working up to a blind rage. Dealing with feelings I don't like and can't stomach. *I feel used.* That's the bottom line. Used and discarded. Wondering how I ever lived alone before her. The whole atmosphere, the space feels so different, empty, quiet and without joy. So after the initial confusion anger came knocking. I'm not a miserable bastard by nature, being anything like my father is something I fought hard against. Easy going came naturally to me though because negativity is poison to the soul. I think that's why I write, because any negative emotions I might contain are released onto paper and not with actual words. Writing them takes away the sting. But being left high and dry does something to me. It's released a side of me that I don't like, don't recognise and I'm not proud of. I need to expel it. The feeling is so unfamiliar that the only way I've managed to deal with it is taking it out on the apartment.

How could she just up and leave? No note, no thanks for the good times, nothing. She won't answer her phone and that's most frustrating of all, she's ghosted me and I have no fucking idea why. Habits are hard to break though and before I leave the bathroom I find myself drawing a smiley for her on the mirror above the cabinet. When I realise she's no longer here to appreciate it I swipe it away and storm from the room.

I find myself in her room and sprawl out on her bed. Her scent lingers everywhere. She really left. And now I'm lost. Who will watch Netflix marathons with me? Who will entertain me with their hideous outfit choices? That was always my most looked forward to part of the day, waiting to see what she'd wander out of her room in. I've never known anyone with such a dedication to onesies. I finally had her, tasted her. I thought we'd finally reached the point where we were honest about our feelings. All the cat and mouse was over or was that just me? I was her first for god sake and whether she admits it or not we connected on a whole other level that night, then she ups and does a runner? Was that it, I scared her off? I feel a strange emptiness. And I realise it's because I was addicted to how she made me feel. I was addicted to who I was when I was around her. Withdrawals are slowly pulling me under.

I roll to my side and open her bedside drawer to find she's left her journals. I never knew what she was writing about but she was more committed than me when it came to getting her word count down. They're all numbered, five in total and I can't resist looking through the pile until I find number one. I hold it for a while telling myself not to do it. *Don't invade her privacy.* How would I feel if she read my manuscript without permission? I tell myself all these things and more but I already know I'm going to open it. I knew the second I found them. Only when I turn the page I realise they were left for me purposely. A yellow post-it note is stuck to the left-hand side, addressed to me.

Dear Ash,

I'm sorry.

Firstly, for leaving you the way I did. Just know if I could have avoided it I never would have left you. Living with you has been the best time of my life.

Secondly, I haven't been completely truthful with you. I always intended to come clean and not in this way but now the decision has been taken out of my hands.

Please read my journals. I hope they will explain what I couldn't bear to tell you in person. I know this is the cowards way out but I've always been better from behind a screen than in person.

I love you and hope one day you'll be able to forgive me.

Fliss

What the fuck is she on about? I read the last line again. We never said those words to one another, but she's written them. She loves me but *left* the first chance she got? Funny fucking way of showing it. My veins have turned to ice and I'm equally reluctant to read more and desperate to. I slowly turn the page, dread creeping in along with my ever-present need for more information.

Diary entry

This is my first journal entry. At the age of 18 I never thought I'd keep any kind of diary but after this week I think it's essential, crucial even. Today my world fell apart. It sounds dramatic to write that but in a way it did. I didn't know there was such a thing as an expiration whilst still living. Today we finally had a diagnosis. For years mum has been more forgetful and not in

the funny way she was when it first started. I used to take the mick out of her, tell her she was getting old, until it stopped being funny and became concerning. Mum became forgetful in a dangerous way. Mum 'morphed' into someone else. She became someone *I* didn't recognise. And now it's her who doesn't recognise me. Mood swings and outbursts became a part of her when all she ever was before was supportive and loving. So when I say my world fell apart, I mean quite literally. Mum was my world and pieces of her started to vanish. My days started and ended with her, she was the best thing about being alive. When they said the words 'aggressive decline' I sat and nodded when all I really wanted to do was jump across the desk, punch him square in the face and scream 'Not my mum!' But that would have been impolite, improper and mum would be mortified to hear of such behaviour. It's funny that I'm still programmed to think how my actions would reflect on her, how disappointed she would be because she hasn't known me for weeks now.

She looks through me, not at me.

She doesn't know she's a mum and that makes the very essence of her gone.

Lost but still here.

Alive but dying.

The woman lying in that bed isn't my mother. She's as much a stranger to me as I am to her. It sounds awful but still true nonetheless. I keep waiting for it to thaw, for her memories to flood through. Just to hear her say my name and look at me with recognition one last time because it happened so quickly. I blinked and she was gone. Vanished before my very eyes. She doesn't speak, doesn't acknowledge me. Her dignity has been stolen. Her expression never changes – she's stuck, somewhere inside and she won't or can't come back. She's living in a body that's fighting to survive. And I don't think she's going to win. So this is why I need to have all my memories written down. If I ever develop Alzheimers like mum then I'll never forget. My life needs to be written down because my future isn't clear and if I'm going to write about my life it needs to be a life worthy of writing about. At the moment it isn't. It's uninteresting, mundane, and there really is nothing to document. If I had Alzheimers it might be a blessing in disguise to forget the life I live. So, from today forward I vow that I'm going to follow all my dreams, I'm going to make my life something worth writing about. Everything that scares me I'm going to achieve. I'm going to fall in love, real love that imprints on your soul and stands the test of time. I won't forget, like I've been forgotten.

I close the book. A lump heavy in my throat. My heart hurts for her. The words jump from the page causing a mirror effect and I feel exactly what she was feeling when she wrote them. My stomach is an empty pit of sorrow – for myself and my loss and for her and hers. I run my fingers over her writing as though I can instill some light in her through her dark.

Jesus. I really know nothing about her. She never spoke about her parents or relatives, about anyone really. We didn't speak about the deep stuff, only skimmed the surface of who we really are.

And now I know why, the topic is just too hard to broach. To voice it is to make it real. To ignore is to forget.

All her frantic writing, while she lived here, makes so much sense. The raw emotion fucking leaping from every confession. These journals were more than just an outlet, they're her life. These thoughts are so personal. She writes them to remember her history, just in case. Because tomorrow's are never promised. These journals are Important and valuable to her, and she left them to me. *Why would she leave something so sacred behind?*

Chapter 12

Felicity

Current mood – Resentful
Regret level - Continuous

D ays have gone past since I left Ash and my happy existence behind. I visit mum every day like the dutiful daughter but I do it out of guilt for deserting her, not because I actually wish to be around her. I hate going and I hate myself for feeling like that but every time I do, I leave with another piece of me missing. I'm resentful, plain and simple. Support groups tell you it's okay to feel this way, that it's natural. But that doesn't lessen the guilt for my impatience with her.

I feel that she's stolen a part of my life and that's partly where the resent comes from. I was always on edge in case people were disapproving or angry towards me. Towards my dwindling empathy. I lacked confidence and assertiveness. It showed in every ounce of my body language. Living with Ash reignited all of it. Living with him helped me reclaim part of who I was before this illness was thrust upon us,it also gave me the opportunity to flourish.

I've lost my compassion. It didn't happen overnight. This was years in the making, mum became someone else, someone unrecognisable over a long period of time. She was never violent until this thing overtaking her brain made her so. She was never volatile, harsh or downright spiteful until one day she was. And the next. Repeated for years. This illness is the cruellest anyone could encounter, but more so for the family left to witness it, because we remember, we know what life was like, what their character once was, their quirks and love for us and now those things are gone replaced by an empty shell. I'm living a new normal but there's absolutely nothing normal about it. I wish there was a quick fix, I searched tirelessly for one. *What good is wealth if it can't buy you more time*?

I turn my phone on seeing 3 texts from Trina, which I reply to with an inadequate 'sorry' and 23 missed calls from Ash. He's persistent I'll give him that, and however much I want to, I can't talk to him. Not until he's aware of how I deceived him and I'll know when he's got to that particular entry. Until then all I can give is radio silence. All I can do is miss him, run myself into the ground with exhaustion to escape the mounting sorrow. I feel spread too thin again, exhausted mentally and can only focus on one negative at a time.

I walk into mum's study, taking a seat behind her desk. Her pride and joy. This was her happy place, where she could read authors manuscripts, find new talent and make their dreams come true. This is where I found Ash' query letter to her, the day I had a definitive diagnosis. I sat in this exact spot going through her papers, trying to concentrate to keep her deadlines going, whilst tears clouded my vision.

His query wasn't exciting enough, it showed none of his personality, which he has in leaps and bounds. If he'd injected even a tenth of it into his letter she would have signed him in a heartbeat. She passed him over because the query didn't pique her interest enough so she didn't even bother to read the first few chapters attached. Or maybe her mind was already too far gone. That infuriated me because his writing was so fresh, if she'd just looked a little closer, *gone deeper* the outcome would have been different. But like I've said, fate has a plan – I still found him, it was just via a different route.

I fire up my laptop and login to Facebook seeing I have messages in my inbox. I'm grateful I can still talk to him through here under the guise of his friend and beta. No contact at all would have finished me off.

Ash: Have you had chance to read over it yet?

Me: I'm sorry but no, I've just sat at my desk now though so will get on it.

Ash: No, don't. Bin it completely. I'm starting from scratch.

Me: What?! Why?

Ash: It was all wrong. I didn't know what I was on about. Now I do. It'll be better.

Me: If you're sure...

Ash: I am.

Me: For a mill would you reconsider?

Ash: Not even for 20 mill

Ashton

Reading Fliss journals are heartbreaking, but they do help with missing her. It feels like we're connecting on another level, sharing your most heartfelt words from your very soul has that effect. I haven't had any answers to whatever she referenced in Journal one as yet but I can't stop reading anyway. Each one gives me more insight into the woman I fell for. They've also been inspiration for turning my novel on its head and making me start from scratch.

I close the book on journal two or is it three? And reach right for the next one.

Dear Journal,
I discovered something today. The publishing industry sucks.
The way they decide whether someones work is worthy
enough by only paying attention to the query is just plain
wrong. Today I read three chapters of an amazing story, I've
taken over whilst mum is... elsewhere and found it whilst
going through her stuff. She noted next to this manuscript that
it was a pass because the query wasn't compelling enough. But

she didn't read the chapters! The story is more than compelling. It angered me so much I did something I shouldn't have – I messaged the author. Found him on social media and stalked his page, luckily for me, due to the backlog at the office he'd never received his rejection. But after waiting way over the deadline for a response he'd gone ahead and self-published. I went straight to the online store selling his book and bought it. I devoured it that night and had to let him know how his words resonated with me and not to give up on his talent. I felt it was my duty to let him know agents aren't always right but since he'd given up on the traditional route anyway I left that out. The author's name is Ashton...

The journal falls from my hand as though it's burnt me. My head starts spinning as I start pacing back and forth. Too much to be a coincidence. *Fliss is Monty*? Monty my beta is Fliss? What the fuck? Did she sucker me in online before suckering me in in person?

I remember that message. It was the first I'd ever received from a reader. Hearing what she thought of my story, my pride and joy was a feeling I'll never experience again. The gratitude I felt that she enjoyed my work so much she just couldn't refrain from reaching out and telling me was tremendous. I spent the rest of that day sporting a shit-eating grin. Knowing I'd touched a reader made me proud, it felt like I'd proven my father wrong, that I was going to succeed.

I can still recount the simplicity of it word for word:

Hi,

I hope this is okay. I've never messaged an author before but wanted to tell you I've just read your book and felt compelled to reach out to you. It had such an impact on me. Thank you for writing it. It truly was a great story.
Monty

Of course, I messaged back thanking her. I knew Monty was female and it was clearly a nickname. And that was it, our friendship was borne. Then it hits me, Fliss Montgomery – Monty, why her surname was so familiar but I couldn't put my finger on it. Her mother, the agent I queried – Montgomery Manuscripts.

I pull out my phone and dial her again. I know it's pointless but the rage I have needs to be expelled. I want answers – from her, not a journal. It goes to voicemail again and I nearly throw my phone, but now I know how to get to her – Facebook and I'll know when she's read the message.

Felicity

Current mood – Despondent
Regret level – Cloudy with a chance of disbelief

I've been spending more and more time in mums study. Some days I just sit here blankly staring. Others I get her affairs in order and sometimes like today when I'm feeling closest to her in her favourite room, I tidy. I found her keys to the different cupboards and drawers she has locks on and have been meticulously organising them ever since.

It's beneficial because these tasks need doing but they're also taking my mind off Ash and the ever-present call I'm expecting from the nursing home.

I pull out another stack of papers along with a binder and place them on her desk. Most will probably need shredding, so I start sorting through them, my eyes skipping over most of the words. One, in particular, catches my eye and I shuffle through the ones behind it, seeing they all have my name on them. I figure it must be her will or something to that effect so start paying attention.

The words jump from the page.

Adoption certificate.

I clench it so tightly that it almost rips. No fucking way. I scan through the rest of it just to appease myself that I have it wrong. That my tired mind is jumping to conclusions. I'm not adopted.

But I am.

All these years, especially the last few when I've been petrified about inheriting this condition because of our shared genes and they never said a word. Never thought it should be something I was made aware of not only on a human decency level but for peace of mind. How could my parents keep something so life-changing from me? How could they let me discover this myself, in this way? Because I have questions, a shit ton of them and neither of them can fucking answer them now. I fall into the seat at the desk, unsure of my next move. I can't demand answers from anyone, I have no one I can cry to or take my frustration out on.

I'm back to being alone and I'm partly to blame for that.

My computer pings.

Ash: All this time its been you?!
I thought you (*Monty*) genuinely liked my book but you're some
kind of psycho bunny boiler with an agenda.

I read it again and again, aware of the fact he can see I've opened it. I knew this day was coming but now it's here I don't know how to respond. My first reaction is to laugh, after what I just discovered, mine and Ash' problems barely scratch the surface. It seems so trivial but I know for him it isn't, he doesn't have other drama in his life, no other deceit can top it for him but fate seems to think I need a plateful of grief.

The discovery I've just made can wait, the call I have to make, can't.

Resigned to this outcome I pick up my phone and dial his number, making the call I've been dreading all along. He answers on the second ring.

"You've got some nerve Fliss!" he rants straight away

"I didn't like it," I shout back. Pissed off at my parents, real and adoptive. He's the closest person to me, even if we aren't very close right now, I still think of him as my person and unfortunately for him, we always take out our problems on those closest to us. I'm also completely infuriated that he'd ever think I lied about that. I know I have no right to be indignant but I am.

"I loved it. You're the only author I've ever reached out to. It had that much of an impact on me. That was never a lie. Believe what you like about my behaviour but I've never been deceitful with my opinions on your craft. I don't know why my *mother* didn't sign you. I would have begged her to if she'd been herself. That's when I started following you when you went the self-published route, that's when I pm'd you. I had to let you know that whatever rejections came your way, they weren't deserved and that you had a fan, a true lover of what you'd written. I never expected you to reply. I never thought we'd become friends and once we did you became important to me. How would you have reacted at that point had I said "By the way I'm the daughter of an agent who shot you down?" You'd have been conflicted. I liked that you spoke to me on an instinctual level because you wanted to not because you might gain from it. I like that you saw me and my worth not my money. Then things went downhill pretty quickly and you were my strength from afar."

"That's what you want to start with? That's the least of my grievances, Fliss."

"Well, it's the least of mine too, Ash. But you brought it up."

"That's it? All you have to say?"

I sigh "I miss you." It just slips out and I know it has no relevance right now but I need him to know it regardless. I miss him so much it hurts to breathe. I'm sad without him, dealing with everything I'm going through alone. Just for a second, I wish he'd say it back.

"You miss me?" he scoffs "You lied to me, used me and then fucking disappeared, Fliss. You left me in limbo. I had no idea what happened to you except for your cryptic fucking clue and these damn journals. You miss me? You have a funny way of showing it."

"I'm sorry, Ash. Truly. I never expected this. I certainly didn't plan to move in with you. I just wanted to meet you. I was desperate and everything ran away with me."

"Yeah, about that. How did you find me?"

"Does it matter?"

"Damn straight it matters!"

"I paid someone to hack you down." I wince at my slip of the tongue. And of course, he doesn't miss it.

"Hack?!"

"Track. I paid someone to track you down."

"You're still fucking lying. Hacking and tracking are two separate things. What the fuck did you hack?"

"I don't know, honestly. I gave some basic information about you and they did the rest."

"What basic information?"

"I ... I read your query to my mum's agency. Your details were on the form."

"How dare you! You could have just asked me. The woman I was speaking to online I'd have loved to meet. She picked me up on some of my worst days, shame you don't stack up in the flesh."

"I was going to tell you. It just got harder and harder to come clean when we..."

"Slept together?" he fumes "Don't romanticise it. It was good, Fliss but it was another lie."

"I was going to say when you started developing feelings..."

"Feelings? You can't develop feelings for a stranger. It was all a lie. Everything I thought I knew and loved about you was fake. I don't know you."

"Yes, you do. Better than anyone. Ash, you have to believe me. I love you and I'm so sorry but if we love each other we can get through anything." I'm begging, knowing he's slipping away from me. I'm desperate and blurting out anything in the hopes he'll change his mind. I've still held on to a crazy notion that he'd be mad but he'd forgive me and beg for me to go back.

"Why would you think that? Jesus Fliss, you're throwing around that word like it's a magic fix. Love isn't the be-all and end-all. It doesn't save everything. Without trust we have nothing. It was all based on a lie. However delicious the intentions, there's no such thing as sweet deceit. I don't even know you so how can I really love you?"

I expected this. Thought I'd prepared myself for it but nothing can really prepare you for the sting of those words, however, deserved they are. He's right though. I was so focused on love I thought it would erode away all deceit but if he doesn't trust me how could we ever work?

I can't speak so I just nod to myself. Today has taken a turn for the worse and I didn't think it could have got any worse. I should have stayed in bed. I take a deep breath and on the exhale I reply "I'm sorry Ash. Truly. I never wanted to hurt you. I knew I would but I really wish I hadn't. Keep reading them, they'll answer so much more than I ever could. You're angry right now and with fair reason to be but... I'll miss you." I linger on the line hoping that he'll say we can work through this. But he never does.

Ashton

"I'll miss you." She says and the line goes dead. I stare at my phone wondering what the hell just happened. How dare she rob me of the chance to confront her face to face. *Is that why she left*? To take the cowards way out? What happened, did she fuck me and then have a hit of conscience? I start pacing around her room like a trapped animal. Everything she's done and lied about just don't add up to the woman I got to know. No one can hide their true self that perfectly.

A text pings and I reach for my phone hoping it's her, I've nowhere near expelled this angry energy and a text row could just help. My hope plummets when I see it's from Trina, she's uncannily on the mark when it comes to getting in touch. Before I sent the Facebook message to Fliss, I rang Trina, gave her the lowdown, let loose some of my rage. I shoot her a quick reply and carry on pacing trying to work off this frustrating energy coursing through my veins.

Moments later my door knocks. I know who it is before I reach it. I imagine her sitting outside just waiting for my SOS. I jog to it, letting Trina in and I don't miss what she's carrying in her hand.

"Ice cream?" I ask

"Why not?" she shrugs "Always worked when we were kids." She walks to my kitchen reappearing with two spoons and sits herself down in Fliss spot on my settee. It's wrong. She's sat there many times since I moved in but never since Fliss did. It belongs to Fliss. Why I give a shit about something so inconsequential is frustrating. She notices me frowning and on an eye roll, she scoots over patting the space beside her for me to join. I remain standing as she whips the lid off the ice cream and dives in.

"So, why the 999?" she asks around a mouthful of raspberry ripple.

"She was a fake. I thought Cammy was bat shit crazy but Fliss takes the crown."

"What are you actually mad about here?"

"Did you not listen to the story?"

"I did, but still go ahead and answer the question."

"All of it."

"No, be specific. Yes, she lied, was deceptive but if you're truthful you don't really care about that. Knowing you it was a huge fucking ego boost knowing that girl wanted to meet you that badly she flew out here just to do it. It was a fucked-up way of going about it no doubt, but you liked her, online and in person. What's the real issue, Ash?

I drop down beside her. I hate how she can read me so well "She left. Left me high and dry, left me wondering whether it was me if she regretted... if I wasn't enough."

"There it is. The whole crux, now you've admitted it to yourself how are you going to handle it?"

"There's nothing to handle, we're done, everything we had wasn't real. She's gone so time to move on and find a way to get over her."

She rolls her eyes "I disagree, that's an excuse. If that was true you wouldn't be so torn up, concerned about whether you were the problem. Everyone deserves a second chance don't they? Seems to me that girl has a lot going on, she needed someone to lean on and chose you, can't blame her for that."

"Can't I?"

"Well, you can, of course. But that's not the Ash I know. You're not heartless. I never told you, but she admitted to me once that she was an awful person. She was torn up over something. I now know that was because she was lying to you and I believe it was genuine. Why do you think she held back so much, kept you at arms length when she clearly only had eyes for you?"

I shrug and shove a spoonful of ice cream in my mouth. I really hate when Trina is fair, logical and can see both sides of the story. She continues anyway "Because she knew this was going to be the end result, there was no way to stop it from coming out. All I can suggest is take some time, don't make lasting decisions based on temporary emotions. Maybe read some more, she left them to you for a reason."

"I hate you." I moan, how can she be so intuitive yet so down on herself?

"Hate you too." She smirks, clinking her spoon with mine before wrapping her arms around me.

After Trina leaves I realise I'm not ready to let my other emotions in, remaining hurt and angry is better, they're emotions I've become more familiar with and accustomed to, I understand them and want to focus on the fact that this all seems premeditated. I still find myself armed with the next Journal though but allow myself based on my inherent nosiness.

Dear ~~Journal~~ Ash

Have you never been desperate? Felt complete and utter despair and that your life was falling apart and no longer in your control? And from that made a bad decision even though you knew it was wrong you continued because it helped you to function? It helped to keep you going, that you had a glimmer of hope and happiness. Your world was no longer governed by pain. I was selfish, I'm more than aware of that but if I hadn't been, I don't think I'd be here now in order to argue with you. I

wouldn't be living if I didn't make that split second decision to chase my future instead of ending my life.

I can't regret that choice.

I didn't realise that by ending my pain I'd be transferring it to you. I have no more words, Ash. I can apologise until my last breath but I know it doesn't make things right. They're just words. My actions from here on out are all I have to prove to you I never wanted to hurt you. People think you can't develop feelings for a stranger but I loved you before we even met. I needed you before I knew how much and I leaned on you when I should have fallen. You made me want to live again. You don't know what a gift that was. You might hate me for deceiving you but I did what I had to to survive. We were meant to meet. If only for you to save a stranger's life... by giving it colour. You kept me going on some of my darkest days. When my mum forgot who I was you stayed up all night with me playing silly games and making me smile through my tears. You never knew that did you? You took my mind off her terrible disease. You made me live, Ash.

Thank you. Those two words are what I should have said to you the moment we met. Thank you for all the distraction from the chaos I was cloaked in. Thank you for sparing my life and thank you for making my dreams come true, if only for a short while. I'll cherish you forever because I owe you so much. If you can't find anything to cherish out of all of this then cherish that. You made someone want to live just by being you. Do you know what a gift that is?

Fliss

Fuck me! A tear falls down my cheek. I'm choked up. I never would have known she was in such a dark place. The Fliss I got to witness was a breath of fresh air but reading what drove her to me, how she wanted to end her life, cuts deep. Reading how she thinks I saved her, how I helped her without even knowing burns deep. I wish I'd known, I would have been a better friend. I could've given her a shoulder to lean on from afar. Hell, I would have travelled to her. That's how much Monty meant to me. I would have done better than the substandard friendship she really received. Her gratitude bowls me over, it's undeserved, my goofing around, taking things for granted were my own coping mechanism – she helped me, online, she was my sounding board, my champion, the driving force for my belief in myself to achieve my dreams.

I get it now. I haven't ever felt that desolate but I know if I did I'd likely react just the same as she did. I'd grasp onto any escape from the torture. I can't blame her for using me as an out. I can't be mad she didn't come clean. Desperation makes people act out of character. The kindest hearts are always the ones that go through the most pain. And my girl has a good heart, one of fucking gold. Her lies could easily erase all that we've shared, but only if I allow it to.

Forgiveness is something I can give her.

Time is something she needs to give me.

Chapter 13

Felicity

Current mood – Devastated
Regret level - Endless

Another month has passed. I've heard from Ash a total of zero times. And today I wish I could lean on him more than ever because that's it. Mum is gone. The only mum I've ever known. And she was a good mum for the most part, if you don't count the lies recently uncovered. I'll never know the circumstances around my adoption from her. I never got to sit with her while she explains how I came to be theirs. Was I unwanted by my birth parents? A secret pregnancy? Did my real parents die? So many unanswered questions that I've left on the back burner. How do you forgive someone for injustices they've caused you? Especially when they're not around to answer for them. To be held accountable. I guess that's the difference, I'm here to be judged for mine and answer to my sins. She isn't and it fucking guts me.

The funeral service went by in the blink of an eye, I think

probably because I was on auto pilot. Just going through the motions. I'm holding everything in because being numb is better than the alternative. The second I let it out it may well be the end of me. I have a tight lid on my emotions right now but they could explode and break free any moment drowning all these people in the torrent.

I smile politely at all the well-meaning strangers in my home. Mum's home. Because it's expected. All here for a free meal, giving me empty words such as 'we're here for you' and 'if you need anything, don't hesitate to ask'. It's laughable because none of these people have the power to grant me the things I want most, yet they act like all I have to do is say the word and they'll fix my universe with a simple click of their fingers.

I could choke from the restriction around my neck. An invisible noose has me in its grasp and I almost like the pain, a tiny bit more pressure and I'd welcome the lights out. Mum's employees, staff, her friends all milling about as though they own the place. It's stifling and every time I see someone do the sympathy smile head tilt, I have to refrain from ramming a finger sandwich down their throat. I don't understand this tradition of a wake. The celebration of someone's life. Why would I celebrate? It seems morose and highly inappropriate but maybe a good excuse to get shit faced.

I've been avoiding making eye contact as that invites conversation. I was never one for small talk and even less so today but all eyes are on me – the orphan. In less than three years I've lost both parents, albeit in different ways. Technically I suppose I've lost four parents in total, but who's keeping count? The pity from these people is overwhelming. I understand this is the done thing but I'm trying desperately not to scream at them all to leave. Today I want the silence. I want and need to mourn, not put on a brave face and endure this farce. I debate whether I can slink off to my room and leave Gerry to socialising but that wouldn't be fair to him. I've already left him to deal with enough.

I make my way to the liquor cabinet, staring at the assortment of bottled numbness. I grab the first bottle I can, taste doesn't matter, I want it for one thing only – the annihilation of my feelings.

"Felicity, I don't think..."

"I don't care what you think, Gerry!" I spin and scream at him, clutching the bottle to my chest as though it's my baby. Heads snap our way and he gently and wordlessly takes my arm leading us from the room, across the hallway to our second reception room.

Once we're alone he wraps me in a tight hug and I don't have the energy to fight him so I let him. I've reverted to my default setting. All the fight I had, has left me. Just another thing to add to my abandonment list. Gerry has been in my life for a long time. He was mums right hand man, he started out here as her PA but his role soon morphed into much more. He's a piece of the furniture now, a surrogate father almost. We've never been particularly close but I appreciate this man more than he'll ever know. Next to me, he loved my mum most. He stepped up when I stepped down, visiting mum everyday, spending hours at a time with her. Doing what I couldn't. If only it was as simple to pay him to take my pain, my regret and all feelings of utter worthlessness, I'd do it in a heartbeat. I thought I'd experienced my heart fracturing before but they were nothing more than the foundations beginning to shift, allowing the ripples to grow over time until there's nothing left but a great gaping hole. One that can't be filled, pasted over or repaired.

"I'm sorry." I murmur against his chest

"Don't be."

"Do you think she knows?" I ask him, pulling back.

He raises greying brows in question "That you left?"

I nod and swallow the lump stuck in the back of my throat.

"She would have understood Felicity, you spread your wings but ultimately I always knew you'd come back. You didn't desert her. You found yourself."

"At her expense." *At his as well. I found myself at Ash' expense. And lost them both.*

He guides me over to a chair and sits facing me "Where you're concerned, she only ever wanted your happiness. If leaving her for a short period of time was what it took to find it, she would have been ecstatic." *That's bullshit and we both know it.* She never wanted me to leave this place, but I allow him to mollify me for his benefit.

"I can't stop thinking about how much time I missed with her all because I was selfish and couldn't handle her illness."

"You handled it for years. Were with her every step of the way. I'd say you deserved a break, needed it, even. Don't ever judge yourself for taking time to consider your own mental wellness."

I scoff at *mental wellness.* My mental state is so defective I should be in a straight jacket, "Did she ever confide in you?"

"Often. Do you mean about something in particular?"

"I've just been wondering about the day she had me, she never told me my birth story. I've wondered why they never had more children, I would have liked siblings. Especially now." I watch for his reaction, waiting for the lies I'm sure are to come.

"Don't ever think you're alone, Felicity. I'm a poor stand-in for both of them, but I am here for you, night or day. Reaching out for help isn't weakness." And there's my answer. Diversion from the question I posed.

But I still cling to him a little longer. I appreciate him a little more. He may not have the answers I need or be willing to tell them to me if he does, but he's the only one around offering comfort and kind words I want to believe. And when we realise how long we've been gone, we pull apart and rejoin the sad affair in the other room.

***

The best part about having staff is that they do everything, all the mundane tasks I've never had to, they're paid to do these things. This is why I can't cook, because we have a chef, why I'm messy – because it always miraculously became tidy again. And now it means I don't have to linger, clear up after all the people have left. I'm able to slink off knowing when I awaken in the morning it'll be like nothing ever happened here. I stumble up our expansive staircase, it looks lovely but is a pain in the arse, especially as it isn't straight. I could navigate my way straight up whilst drunk but this winds around, causing me to stumble. I grip the balustrade as I try to keep my balance and just for a second I stay rooted in place wondering if I fell, would it really be that bad?

I stay paused considering the idea for a few moments but realise I'd likely only end up with broken bones prolonging the pain I'm already in. *Not* ending it.

I push off and sway again as I make my way to my room and once I reach it I collapse to the floor because after all that exertion making it to the bed isn't an option.

Sleep claims me quickly, mercifully and there's nothing but darkness. For once I'm allowed some respite from my dreams.

I'm wrapped in strong arms, my nostrils invaded by a glorious scent, one that is so, so familiar. Held as though I weigh nothing. I'm floating and breathe in deeply, letting the smell calm me. Letting the comforting thought of him being here with me engulf me.

I'm placed in my bed and feel it dip as he joins me.

I latch on to his arm "Stay with me." I beg

"I will. I'm here and not going anywhere."

"How are you here? Did I sleepwalk all the way to you?"

He laughs and I feel immediately lighter. That is a sound I never thought I'd be lucky enough to hear again. Ash is a tonic, he feeds my soul happiness.

"This time, I tracked you down."

"I'm not allowed boys in my bedroom," I tell him

Another laugh "Good job I'm not a boy then."

"Mum is really strict about…" I trail off remembering house

rules no longer apply because the one who set them is no longer around to enforce them. I start to cry. *A grief surge.* That's what the support groups call it. A grief surge is a literal hit of grief. They can come from nowhere but the pain it strikes into you is frighteningly deep. Something as simple as a sound, smell, picture, or phrase can bring one on. Triggers are everywhere.

I can't hold it in any longer, the alcohol has lost its edge, I'm dreaming that Ash is holding me and finally I can unleash it all. My body wracks with the strength of my sobs. I'm really and truly alone in this world. The last person that loved me unconditionally is gone. What will I do without her?

He smoothes the hair from my face, gently shushing me, whispering endearments as his arms remain wrapped around my fetal position "Let it out, Fliss. I've got you."

When I wake the following day, I turn to see if he was imagined. There's nothing but an empty space beside me so I scream into my pillow as I punch it repeatedly. It really was a dream. My throat hurts so I sit up hoping I was wise enough last night to bring water with me. I look around my room but I find none, instead, my eyes fall to something propped on my vanity unit. Stacks of white paper, a yellow post-it note attached to the front.

I creep towards it as though it's a message from the grave. Something mum left behind for me to read over. When I realise it isn't her handwriting but the lazy scrawl of Ash' I wonder for a second if this is some kind of peace offering, maybe he wants me to beta for him again. Gerry must have left it here for me to find.

I peel the note off:

Read me, then finish me.

Our story isn't over yet but I'm going to need your help writing our ending.

Title: Sweet Deceit.

Authored by: Ashton Blake and Felicity Montgomery

My hand flies to my mouth. He was here. He really came to me when I needed him most. I spin around searching for him, hoping he'll be stood behind me. He isn't. I sink to my floor clutching the manuscript he left behind, a weeping mess. He wrote *our* story?

I crawl my way back to bed and climb in. I turn the first page and the dedication brings me to tears. It's my favourite quote by Harvey Mackay, the one I took quite literally when I embarked on my crazy scheme to fly to Ash. After each line he's added his own words:

Everything happens for a reason. - *Fate decides.*

If you get a chance take it. – *She did*

If it changes your life, let it. – *I did*

Nobody says it will be easy. – *Ain't that the truth.*

They just promised it would be worth it. – *And it was. It is.*

I can't read any further for the tears clouding my eyes and the restriction in my chest. He took my favourite quote and applied it to us. Tweaked and adapted each line to hold even more meaning. He altered it for this crazy situation I created.

I discard the papers and drag myself from the bed. I feel gross and just want to shower my sadness away. I head towards my en suite, opening the shower door as I turn it on and adjust the temperature. I turn around to study my tear-streaked face and that's when I see it.

My shower smiley with a difference.

The mirror is completely covered in yellow post-it notes all with an array of smileys drawn on them. A visual display of happiness, but Ash being who he is threw in some deformed drawings to mimic my lame attempt at them.

I peel one off and turn it over because I can see through that something is written there.

Breathe.

I pull another and then another, each one with a different written message of encouragement.

Keep moving

Be strong

Eat

Find me

I let each one flutter to the ground.

He is here. Where? I forgo the shower in favour of hunting him down. I've been without him for far too long. He's been here but is he still? Gerry must have let him in, he's the only other person left to roam this place. His quarters are separate from the main house but I have a feeling he's been staying here recently, unwilling to be too far away in case I needed him.

I practically sprint down the staircase, through the hallway, looking into rooms as I pass. I come skidding to a halt when I reach the kitchen.

The sight of him in my home is mesmerising. He's leaning against a countertop, arms crossed. Relaxed in a grey tee and sweats. A complete sight for sore eyes. Neither of us move as we take one another in. I'm hesitant to go to him, after our phone conversation and complete silence from him afterwards I'm not sure of his intentions here. Maybe he's realised he just wants me as a friend and is being a good one coming to offer comfort. I can't stand the idea he might just be here out of pity. I left the journals so the truth would be known without my having to fess up, not so he could feel sorry for me. They weren't an excuse for my actions. They were the reason. Simple as. I want a lot from him but pity isn't on the list.

He opens his arms and I can't stop myself from running to them, wrapping myself in him.

"Thank you." I murmur against him as he strokes my hair comfortingly.

"Don't thank me, Fliss. Not for being here for you. I should have come sooner."

"I can't believe you're really here, after..."

He cuts me off, "It doesn't matter. Life's too short, right?"

"But... you can't just forgive and forget."

"You feel that?" he whispers, pressing up against me.

I do feel it. My eyes concentrate on the rise and fall of his chest before I flick my eyes up to his "Your heart? All that proves is you're alive, congratulations!" I pull back trying to stay composed, trying to keep some distance by being contrary because I don't feel I deserve his forgiveness. I'll beat myself up over it forever. Just as I pull away he grasps my hand and spins me back to him.

"*You* make me feel alive." He places my palm over his chest "It only beats like this when you're near."

I let my head drop. Tears are threatening to fall and I yell at them in my head to freeze. Eye leakage at this moment in time is not only unwanted it's completely unhelpful because he'd wrap me in those arms and they'd never stop. My throat is battling a lump that I'm struggling to swallow past. He means every word. This isn't Ash messing with me, this is him being real. I let his words wash over me, savouring them for only a second, whilst my heart falls at the sincerity. Knowing I don't deserve them is killing me. A while ago I would've given my soul to hear words like this, but now, now the guilt consumes me. I've won and lost all in one.

Happiness can't be built on a cocktail of fantasy and lies.

Why I ever thought it could is beyond me.

"Let it go, Fliss. Stop holding it over yourself. I forgive you. Now you need to."

Ashton

I've processed my anger. Overanalysed and dissected what she did and now I'm healed... partially. She has bigger things to be concerned about right now. I'm here for her in all ways. To lean on, to cry to and to take her snarkiness, anger, and emotional breakdowns. I'll put up with it all, but I won't let her beat herself up over something that now feels so meaningless. I will not allow her to push me away again, not now she's finally admitted her feelings. Not now I know the truth she was hiding. She can't run this time. I'm armed with all the facts and I still want this. Us. I can't let her pretend she doesn't because of some misplaced guilt. I finally understand what pushed her to that sweet deceit.

"It's that simple for you to forgive me?" she asks wide-eyed as though she's waiting for the punch line.

"Yes."

"You don't have any resentment towards me?" her eyes narrow. *So suspicious, Fliss.*

"Zero," I tell her

She shakes her head. Still unsure, wary.

"How can I convince you?"

"You already have. I was pushing for kicks." She smiles up at me and I'm blown away. Even now as fragile as she is she's still giving me what I need, this playfulness that is us in all our glory.

I pull her back against my chest "I missed you."

"Not as much as I missed you, Ashton," she whispers

"I beg to differ."

"Beg all you like, you're wrong if you think otherwise."

I engulf her, pressing my lips to hers, making her jerk at the contact before she melds against me. I pull away earning me a confused frown.

"You need to eat, Fliss. You've lost so much weight." She was always slim, but now she's verging on underweight. She looks gaunt, and although the loss of a parent could be a good cause for this, I know it isn't. This has been weeks in the making, of not looking after herself and having no one to look after her when she was incapable of doing so.

"I'd rather just be in your arms."

"Food first, then I'll hold you all day and night."

"I'm not hungry, Ash. I don't need a lecture right now so if that's why you're here..."

"You want me to go?" I challenge "Say it and I will."

She drops her head "No, I don't want you to. I'm sorry, I'm a mess. I just... I'm angry and sad and then you're here and I'm happy. It's too many emotions to process. I don't know how I'm supposed to act. What am I supposed to do?" she whispers on a sob.

"Take it one day at a time, baby. I'm here for you. I've got you,"

Chapter 14

Fliss

Current mood – Fatigued
Regret level – Holy shit I fucked up

I spend the rest of the day in bed wrapped in his arms, apologising repeatedly, crying and drifting in and out of sleep. I can't believe how lucky I am. A small part of me still believes he's here for moral support, to comfort me in the aftermath of my mothers passing, that he's such a good guy he'd fly to be with me in a time like this, so selflessly despite my lies and what I made him feel. A larger part of me feels relief and gratefulness I can never repay. Without him coming to my rescue I'm sure I would have crumbled by now. In between sleeping I've been reading our story, at the moment it's all from Ash's point of view and it's beautiful, reading how he felt when he first met me, what living with me was like, what he enjoyed most about our time together. I'm only halfway through so know the toughest part to read is yet to come but reading this from his perspective is a much-needed confirmation, to know his feelings matched mine and he was as frustrated by the situation as I was is a relief. This is something else he's given to me, wanting me to add to the story from my POV, giving me something to keep busy, to take my mind off all that's happened.

I've never wanted to write my own story, always been happier to read other peoples work, but this is a gift I can't turn down and I want him to be able to read my no holds barred truth.

"I've run you a bath." He says reappearing from my en suite

I smile weakly, not sure I have the energy to walk across the room but also knowing I stink to high heaven and he's probably desperate to be rid of smelly Fliss, seeing as I've been wrapped around him all day.

I throw the covers back, gingerly climb out of bed and make my way across the room. My sight is slightly blurry but I shrug it off and hug him "Thank you." I say as I make my way past him to the bathroom.

I strip off, climb in and immerse myself in the heat and bubbles, wrapping my arms around my legs and letting my silent tears fall. Wishing that grief wasn't an emotion that existed. I wash and then lie in my water cocoon until the water goes cold.

I drag myself from the warmth, wrap the towel he left around me and sway on my feet. I feel dizzy and lean against the wall until it passes. *I really should have eaten when Ash told me to.*

I push away from the safety of the wall, take a step forward and the world goes black.

When the world comes back into focus I realise I'm in hospital, the clinical feel, sound of machines and fetching gown I'm wearing are all big clues. Ash darts forward in his chair and is by my side, clasping my hand in an instant.

"Thank God." He says as he takes my hand and pulls himself closer. He looks dishevelled and drawn. Worry etched all over his handsome face.

"What happened?" I ask him

"You passed out, remember?"

I shake my head.

"You fainted in the bathroom and hit your head. You've been in and out of consciousness, that's why we brought you in."

"We?"

"Gerry and I."

I bring my hand to the side of my head, wincing as I touch the lump that's throbbing. That'll explain my headache from hell. I look back to Ash and being unused to seeing his usually carefree features morphed into concern I play down how I feel, "I'm just tired, Ash. I haven't eaten, I felt a little faint but just need food."

The door opens before he can reply and in walks a nurse. Ash jumps to his feet.

"Hello, Felicity. Nice to see you're back with us. How are you feeling?"

"A little silly to be honest. This is all because I haven't eaten."

She nods as she looks down at my chart. When she returns her gaze to me she says "Felicity, we ran some tests." Her gaze flicks over at Ash before continuing "Would you mind if I speak to Felicity privately, please?"

I can see he's about to argue having to leave me, so step in "It's okay, I want him here. Is something wrong?"

I don't remember hearing the next sentence, because of a sudden whooshing in my ears. My mind settles only on four words ricocheting around my head as I register Ash' reaction. That's how I know I didn't imagine them.

Ash has quite literally turned ashen. He sways a little on his feet. I can't help him though. I have no words either, the shock has rendered me speechless. My throat is completely dry. The four words ringing in my head *"The baby is fine."*

Ashton

The nurse leaves and I fall into a chair, my head swimming with the news she just dropped on *Fliss. Pregnant.* My mind flashes back to the one and only night we spent together, remembering that I never suited up. *No glove, no love.* It's been my motto since I was old enough to be sexually active. But that night was so unexpected, so wanted that in the heat of the moment I got caught out. I have no doubt the baby she carries is mine, what I doubt is whether I can do this.

We haven't spoken, clearly shock has set in, rendering us both speechless. My relief that Fliss wasn't seriously ill was quickly replaced by fear. I look over to her, she's paler now than she was before. This is a clusterfuck of epic proportions.

Suddenly, as though she's only just processed what is happening, she slaps a hand over her mouth "I got drunk." She says

I frown "What do you mean, Fliss?" I have no idea what her train of thought is.

"Mums funeral. I got wasted, you found me on the floor. I'm pregnant and I drank."

"It's okay. The nurse said the baby was fine, remember. I'm sure a couple of drinks won't matter, it's not like you've been regularly drinking is it?"

She doesn't answer my question and I'm not sure if that's because she has been drinking frequently, because she didn't hear me or if she's simply avoiding answering.

"I don't want a baby."

The sentence hangs in the air like a bad smell.

Well shit. I didn't want a baby either. I imagined when I was ready to be a dad I'd be married and it would be something we'd discussed and planned. I thought when the time came I'd be in a place where I could afford to have a child. This was never in my immediate future but years down the line. Hearing her say she doesn't want one, present tense unsettles me though. We may not have planned for this but she's carrying my child, someone I helped create and until this very moment I didn't know how much I craved this.

Timing is shit, our relationship, if it can be called one is up in the air. We've known one another in person for months, hardly the basis we should be building a future on. We're still figuring out us. I mean we don't even live in the same country. If I'm reeling then she definitely must be, still recovering from her fall, her grief because if she's concerned about the alcohol she put in her system whilst pregnant, it must mean she's already protective of the life growing inside her. Maybe without realising she wants this baby more than she knows.

"I think maybe we should let it sink in. You've had a lot happening the past few days, you need to rest and take care of yourself first and foremost. Everything else can wait, okay?"

"I'm so sorry, Ash. I never meant to trap you. I didn't put two and two together. I can't believe I'm pregnant."

"Shhh, it took two of us Fliss, you're no more at fault here than I am."

The car journey back to Fliss' home after being discharged is spent in silence, Fliss curled into my side. Gerry who is driving, frequently looks in the mirror, thinking he's checking on her discreetly. Turns out this guy I was so threatened by is old, was never a threat and really is an employee of Fliss'.

I had a lot of convincing to do before he let me set foot in the house the day I showed up after the funeral, which by the way was another shock. Fliss family home is huge, she clearly comes from money and whilst I do too, seeing her wealth is something else. Like her, I'll also only have my family's wealth at my disposal by inheritance and I'm happy to never get it if it means they need to die for me to do so. I know Fliss would give it all up to be dirt poor if it meant getting her mother back. Especially now, when she's going to be a mother herself.

My head is spinning. Everything has happened so fast. Truth be told I wasn't quite over her betrayal but once I found out about her mother it forced my hand and spurred me forward to make my move. We may not have spent years together getting to know one another like most couples who date do, but we lived together, we bonded before that online and I've been privy to her innermost thoughts from reading and re-reading her journals. *Can we work?* Especially now that our relationship is moving at the speed of a freight train with our unexpected news.

The car pulls to a stop and neither of us moves. It's as though once we do we'll have to face this reality and neither of us is prepared for it. The door opens and I look out to see Gerry patiently waiting for us to make a move. Fliss pulls away from me and allows him to guide her out and up the steps to the front door. I wait a beat, take a deep breath and follow.

I feel like a spare part. Gerry escorted Fliss to her room, me traipsing behind and once she was inside he left. Fliss crawls beneath her covers and turns so her back faces me. I want to say something, talk to her, rid this uneasiness in the air. But nothing comes to mind. I pick up the manuscript sitting on her bedside table and leave quietly.

Felicity

Current mood - Disappointed
Regret level – 100x3000 divided by 9 with a pickle on top

I'm pregnant, echoes in my head. The first time I have sex and I'm stupid enough to do so without protection. If my mother was here she'd be so disappointed in me. I'm disappointed in myself.

How stupid could we be? The fact she isn't here to show her dissatisfaction is another silver lining I guess.

I don't know how long I've lain here thinking through every option but I've at least reached a decision.

I pick up my phone and dial my doctor.

Ash will thank me in the long run. He never wanted this, he'd stick by me out of a sense of duty but if given a choice he'd have wanted to wait. I've forced him into so much already. I know if I spoke to him about his feelings on the subject he'd tell me what he thinks I want to hear. Deceit seems to be my thing so why stop now?

I feel better now the pain meds are working and a decision has been reached. I slip from the bed and go in search of him. Finding him sat at the breakfast island writing furiously.

"Hi." I say meekly

He swivels around on his chair and offers up a small smile "Hi."

I pull up a seat next to him, glancing at the pages spread over the unit. "Adding to our story?" I ask

He looks sheepish "I thought my part was over but... I needed to get something else down."

"Our pregnancy shock?"

"Yeah, are you okay with that?"

"I guess. I mean it is part of our ongoing story. I hadn't finished reading it though. Will be doing alternating points of view throughout – your take and then mine to see how they coincided?"

"Sounds good to me and will flow better. Do you really want to talk about this though?"

I sigh "Was better than awkward silence, wasn't it?"

"I think the awkward silence was preferable to conversation filler that is so irrelevant right now. We have to face this. I need to know where you're at and you need to know where I'm at."

"Go ahead."

He rubs his jaw before letting his eyes meet mine "I know this was a shock, we didn't plan for this and may not have wanted it to happen this way, but I want this baby." He blows out a breath as though that was a weight off his mind, admitting that out loud.

"Why do you want it?" I ask, needing to hear a valid reason other than now it's happened we'll deal with it. He frowns at my question.

"Why? Because we created a life, we can't just extinguish it because it doesn't fit in with our goals."

"Are you religious, Ash?"

"Not particularly, but I don't agree with abortion as a goddamn contraceptive."

"But you believe having a child that isn't wanted is better?"

"Not wanted? I just told you it is wanted."

"By you."

"Why don't you want this?" he asks

"For so many reasons, more reasons than because we're lumbered with this now so deal with it. We have choices now."

"I don't know you at all do I?" he accuses angrily

"I guess not. We jumped into this guided by feelings and emotions, we haven't used our heads. I haven't been sensible, I let myself get carried away with spontaneity for the first time in my life and look what I've achieved. I lied to you, I left my dying mother alone and now I've ended up pregnant. None of them were smart choices. None of them were thought through and they are all mistakes I regret hugely."

"You regret meeting me?"

I shake my head "I regret the tactics I used to do so."

"Good, that means you have a conscience. And I'm begging you to think of that conscience now. Could you get rid of this baby and live with the decision, without beating yourself up? Without feeling guilty? Without wondering everyday whether it would have been a girl or a boy? Without wondering if we'd have been even happier together as a family? Could you live with whatever the consequences of your actions will be?"

"I don't know, Ash. I can't see into the future. I can only control the here and now. I've been so focused on what was out of my control that everything I've done to escape that, to pretend like I was in control made everything worse. I won't be coerced into doing something I don't feel ready for or equipped to handle."

"Neither of us are ready for this, but we'll learn together. You won't be figuring this out alone. You're not alone anymore, Fliss. I'm here, I'm willing and ready to take on any weight you need removed from your shoulders. We can do this, but only if we do it together."

My head drops "I'm scared." I admit on a whisper

"Me too, babe. We can be scared together."

"This is huge, Ash."

"We haven't exactly been conventional from day one have we? Why would we start now?" he leans forward, wrapping his hands in my hair and kisses my head.

"Ouch." I yelp as his fingers graze my lump.

"Shit, I'm sorry. For a moment I forgot you had a banged-up head. Want me to kiss it better?"

"Hell no. Leave my bump alone."

His eyes flick down to my stomach, he places a hand over it. "The next bump you have will be showered with kisses constantly."

"Ash I…"

"I know. You haven't agreed to anything yet. Give me a chance to wear you down. I'll convince you this will be a good thing. The smartest choice you've ever made."

"I thought you were the smartest choice I've made."

"Oh I was, and lucky for you I came as a two for one deal."

"This was the weirdest buy one get one free purchase I ever made," I mumble

He grins as he senses my wavering decision.

"Are you really ready for this?"

"I'm always ready. You know that." He winks

The next few days pass with Ash distracting me from my grief, my pain, and my nausea in any way he can. My doctors appointment was put on hold and I can't say being spoilt and waited on by him are things I don't like. I may love him but more than anything I'm grateful for him. I think that maybe the thing most overlooked in relationships. When we get bogged down by everything else, our gratitude for our other half is rarely spoken of or acknowledged. The little things they do to make our lives easier is taken for granted. I never want to do that. We haven't broached how long his visit here will last, we're taking the days one at a time. But it's a constant niggling aggravation in the back of my mind. He will have to leave and with him gone I'm worried I'll waver.

I'm sat in my living room, adding my parts to Ash and I's story when I see Gerry saunter past, straight-backed as always, making his way to our front door. I have zero interest in whoever might be calling so I get back to my writing. This manuscript isn't far off being finished and I can't wait for this to be my first project with what has become my publishing company. I'm going to make sure the representation Ash receives is second to none. He deserves his work to be seen and to reach as many readers as humanly possible. His sections of this are so poignant whilst adding a comedy edge to them. His talent is enviable. If anything lets this story down it will be my writing and influence in it.

I whip my head up as I realise a heated exchange is going on in my hallway. Unable to resist I edge my way to the living room door and peek my head around the corner. I can't see who the caller is because of the way the door opens and Gerry's body blocking out the entry. But I can hear.

"I want my money, Gerry! We have an agreement and she's breaking the terms of it." A woman shrieks.

Uh Oh, what the hell has Gerry got himself into.

"Jesus, Millie. She's passed away. We're still getting all her affairs in order."

This has my attention. They're talking about my mother, not some gambling debt or something else Gerry forgot to pay off, but money my mother owes?

"She's dead?" The woman asks in disbelief "Surely provision was made for circumstances such as this?"

"I'm sure they were, but..." he lowers his voice and I have to strain to hear his reply "... the girl doesn't know and she's taken over."

"Really? Maybe it's time she was enlightened then?"

"Don't even think about it. You agreed to the terms if you break your silence the deal is null and void."

"I need that money, Gerry. I suggest you fix this, however you have to to ensure it's mine by the end of the week. Deal or not, I'll sing like a bloody canary if it isn't in my account."

They're so focused on their arguing viewpoints, Gerry's body angled mostly out of the door, that they don't hear my approach. Gerry's knuckles are white from the grip he's maintaining on the door. I pull it back further, away from him, causing his arm to drop and he spins to face me. I, however only have eyes for the woman standing on my threshold.

She looks me up and down and as she does her features soften ever so slightly. Her hand flies to her mouth as she gasps.

"Can I help you?" I ask her

She shakes her head, her eyes flicking behind me to Gerry.

"Are you sure? Because I don't appreciate my staff being threatened. If my mother had some sort of business transaction with you that I've fallen behind on, then I'm the only one who can release funds."

Her eyes water, something akin to shame passes over her face and without another word, she turns on her heel and walks away. I watch her go, taking in her expensive shoes, tailored trousers, and fitted coat. Her blonde bob bounces as she strides away and I can't tear my eyes from her. She never spoke a word to me, yet her silence is more than telling.

Gerry clears his throat behind me and I spin around to train questioning eyes on him. He looks guilty, resigned to coming clean, about what, I don't know.

Before closing the door and starting my interrogation, Ash comes bounding up the steps, a bunch of flowers in his arms, a wide grin aimed at me which quickly falters as he nears. He reaches me and kisses my cheek "Hey babe, what's wrong? Morning sickness again?"

I incline my head in the direction of the sitting room and lead the way, expecting that they'll follow.

They walk in behind me, looking like naughty schoolboys about to be reprimanded by the head teacher. I indicate for Gerry to sit across from me and pat the space next to me for Ash to claim. He passes me the flowers he's still holding and silently sits.

"What was that about?" I ask Gerry

"Felicity...I..."

"What, Gerry? Was mum into something dodgy? Let me guess... was she a drug mule? Or maybe she hired a hit on someone?"

Ash bursts out laughing but one look at my unamused expression and he goes silent.

"Felicity, your mother... purchased something from that woman, something of the highest value. An instalment agreement of sorts was put in place. Your mother has never missed a payment... until now."

"Okay, so what did she buy? Tell me where to find the agreement and I'll honour it."

He bows his head "I'm in somewhat of a dilemma. Your mother never wanted you to know about this. I gave my word I'd protect it."

"What's with all the cloak and dagger? What the hell did she buy, Gerry?" Ash rests a hand on my jiggling leg as my voice raises. I feel like I need a drink. I know I'm not going to like the answer because goosebumps have sprouted all over my body.

He looks crestfallen, but on a resigned sigh he looks me dead in the eye and whispers "You. She bought you, Felicity."

Chapter 15

Felicity

Current mood – Out of body experience
Regret level – Math I can't do

Laughter pours from my mouth. That's the most ludicrous thing I've ever heard. People like my parents don't buy children. I never knew Gerry had such a warped sense of humour. Yet, this is more distasteful than anything. I look from him to Ash, neither of them are so much as smiling. I wonder briefly if I'm having some sort of sleepwalking episode.

"Am I awake?" I ask Ash

He nods sombrely "I'm afraid so." He replies

I cut my gaze to Gerry who is squirming uncomfortably "This isn't a sick joke?"

"I wish it was, Felicity."

I jump to my feet and start pacing around the room, my heart and breaths coming erratically, "Gerry this isn't funny. What the hell are you saying? I was sold? You're telling me I'm nothing more than a transaction? What the actual fuck?!"

"Language!" Gerry reprimands

"Fuck off," I scream at him.

"Fliss..." Ash starts

"What, Ash? Calm down? Don't even think to say that to me right now. Would you be calm? Is there a certain way information like this should be received? Oh wait, I was never meant to know, was I?"

He stands and strides to me, ignoring my tirade. He wraps me in his arms and we just stand like this in the middle of the room while my world comes crashing down for the second time. I sob against him.

"Who does that?" I ask angrily as I pull away, swiping at my tears and stare down at Gerry "What was I worth?"

He looks away as though doing so will make me leave well alone. "Answer me, Gerry. What was paid for me? How much did that woman – my birth mother sell me for? Pennies? Pounds?"

"I don't know." He answers

"I don't believe you for a second"

His guilt isn't as strong as his dedication and allegiance to my mother, for a moment I think he's going to open up but then his head drops and I know I'm in this alone. Loyalty to mother wins.

" Fine, then I'll tear this place apart, there must be statements, you mentioned an agreement. If there's proof to be found I'll bloody well find it." I stand, throw my flowers at him and storm from the room, heading to my mother's study. The bundle of information I found, including my adoption certificate, was placed back in a draw and I never looked into them any further. They're my starting point.

I hear Ash enter behind me as he closes the door.

"Jesus, Fliss. I don't know what to say."

"Don't talk then, help me look." I throw over my shoulder as I round the desk and rifle through the drawer.

"Do you really want to do this? Digging deeper might not help."

"Nothing will help, but I'll be armed with the facts and that's better than being in the dark."

I find the pile I was looking for and instead of sitting at the desk chair, I wander to the middle of the room and lay them on the floor in front of me as I sit cross-legged. Ash joins me and together we go through them.

"This says you were adopted." He says holding up the adoption certificate

"Yeah, I know. At least something was legal." I snort

"Gerry!" I yell and moments later he enters looking sheepish. I know this isn't his fault, but he was privy to this information and is the only one who can answer my questions.

"I want to know how this came about. I have the adoption certificate, so was something drawn up alongside it? I want the whole truth from start to finish."

"May I sit?" he asks pointing to the couch behind me

"Go ahead."

Once seated, he thinks for a moment, wondering how to begin, probably also wondering how this responsibility fell to him.

"The woman who arrived here earlier is called Millie. She took on a cleaning position here 20 years ago. Your mother and father were having trouble over their inability to conceive. From what I understand, Millie and your father started an affair that resulted in her becoming pregnant. Your father was overjoyed that he would finally be a father but fearful for he knew that was the ultimate deception. An affair your mother may have forgiven, but one that resulted in a child would be more than she could bear.

Millie had other ideas, though. She was your age and a baby was the last thing she'd planned for. She told your father in no uncertain terms that she would not be keeping the child. He threatened her and in retaliation, she went to your mother and told her the whole sordid affair. Your mother was heartbroken, as you can imagine. She sacked Millie and threw her out. After having time to digest what she'd learnt, she rang Millie and asked to meet with her, which is where they came to an agreement if Millie carried the baby to full term, your mother would adopt the child and set Millie up for life with monthly payments on the condition that she never made contact with you, never made herself known in any way, shape or form, and this payment would run until you reached 21."

I shake my head "So, once I reached that age, she could have just walked up to me in the street and introduced herself? My parents were never going to forewarn me?"

"I'm sorry, Felicity, I really don't know all the ins and outs. All I know is the history."

"Where did she find the strength to do that? How could my mother agree to raise a child who was a result of an affair he had?"

"She loved him, she wanted him to be happy and managed to put his wants and needs before her own. She couldn't carry a baby for him, but she could raise a baby with him."

"Un-fucking-believable!" Ash says as he rubs my back.

"I can't believe this." I say as a wave of nausea rolls over me, I jump up and run from the room straight to the nearest toilet.

I wondered where my deceptive streak came from because my parents were always pillars of the community in my eyes. This proves otherwise. I was always screwed because nature and nurture both fucked me over. I dry heave as my throat burns. I don't know if this is from shock or from the life growing inside me. What I do know is the apple doesn't fall far from the tree because I'm the same age as my birth mother when she fell pregnant and I'm also carrying a child I don't want. This just cements my decision, although I would never sell a child.

I lean back on my heels, running through my entire life in my mind. Everything I knew and believed has been shattered to smithereens. My whole identity is in question and I don't know how to make peace with that.

I make my way back to the study, walking in on Ash and Gerry having a heated debate. They stop the moment they realise I'm back.

"That's why my mother brought me up the way she did. Like I was a duty, she was kind to me, but always held me at arms length. She raised me to rely on her, to be my world because she knew I wasn't really hers and she craved the devotion whilst loathing it because I was a constant reminder of my dad's affair. She loved and resented me. But she paid for the privilege, was saddled and was going to get her worth out of me."

"That's not true, Felicity," Gerry says jumping to my mother's defence as always, even now after telling me this farce of a story, she can do no wrong in his eyes.

"Isn't it? She never did anything with me, never played games, taught me to bake, took me on shopping trips or holidays. I was a prisoner in this house, I wasn't even allowed to go to school, but taught here by tutors instead. She provided for me, but now I think about it she wasn't maternal. I always thought she was my best friend, but it's because I had no one else. She was literally my all because she excluded me from mainstream life. I wasn't her all though, I was her lot in life. Brought up to have an education but not so I could have my pick of jobs, so I could take over her company, still keeping me chained to her."

"She loved you, Felicity. You have to believe that."

"I'm sure she did, in her own way. But don't you see, she couldn't love me properly. Especially as she did this all for my dads happiness and he still left her anyway. Left her to look after his child he persuaded her to bring up."

"She kept this from you to spare your feelings."

I snort "I hate her. I'm glad I left her."

"Don't say that."

"Why, it's the truth."

His eyes flick to the door, no doubt planning his escape, wondering if it's acceptable for him to leave now he's played his part "I know this has been a shock. I'm going to leave you to digest it, unless there's anything else you want answered?"

"I want that woman's name, address, and phone number."

"Whatever you need." He agrees, before making a hasty exit.

Betrayal leaves a mark, like a blemish on the skin, only this goes beyond skin deep. In time it might fade or in turn, it can ultimately become a scar. A constant reminder of the wrong served. I don't want to allow this to fester and turn into an ugly scar. I know to achieve any kind of closure I'll have to tackle it head-on. Speak to Millie and lay this all to rest. Because I have my own life to live. There are no more secrets or skeletons in my closet. If anything, this explains so much and while I'm pissed off how I was used like an item you'd buy at a supermarket I've been through worse. I will get through this, I have to because curling up and whining about the unfairness won't bring me peace. It won't change what happened. The only positive about this whole situation is that I was looked after, fed, clothed, educated. I didn't end up being bought by people to be enslaved or used. I was never beaten. I just was. I existed. Life is so much more than that. Feeling love, loss and laughter are things we have to go through. Never having any heightened emotions of any kind isn't healthy – but that's what I lived with, until mums illness. That was the first time in my life I've ever had to wade through strong, confusing emotions and thought processes that were alien to me. It was the first time I had to step up. They woke me up to my robotic routine, my empty life.

I'm all for new experiences but meeting my real mother, the woman who sold me at birth is an experience I don't know how to prepare for. I'm angry but numb.

Anger is easier to hold on to. Compassion, empathy, any kind of understanding takes more work than allowing anger to take centre stage. Anger is an old friend, I'm just hoping I can make it past this step and get to the complacency level.

Ashton

"Fliss, you look exhausted. Come and lie down. Remember you're carrying precious cargo now. I want you both healthy."

"About that..." she starts and my heart falls "Never mind." She says and for once I don't push her because I know what she was about to say would break my heart. I'm attached to our baby already. I'm excited now, baby names are on my brain constantly.

"Been a long day, huh?" I ask as she presses into my side

"Ash, my family dynamics are crazy. Are you sure you want to stick around?"

"All families are messed up. It's not your family I love, anyway, it's you. You can't scare me off."

"What if you found out I used to be a man?"

"That's not the first time you've made reference to being male. I have to say though, if you were, the surgeons did a bloody good job on you."

"Tell me something about you that I don't know." She asks, looking up at me.

"I've been having parent troubles too," I admit as I brush her hair away from her face.

She wriggles in my arms "You have? Why what's wrong?"

"Long story short?"

She nods, eager for more information about me, "Well, like your mother, my dad had the crazy notion that I'd work for him and one day take over the business. When I told him I wanted to be a writer... we had words which caused a rift. The apartment was a gift, originally. He bought it and presented it to me for my birthday but as soon as I didn't do what he wanted, didn't adhere to the path he set out for me, he told me I have to pay for it – which is why I needed a onesie wearing flatmate."

She hugs me tighter, and stares up at me, "I knew fate was on my side. My shitty news about my mum led me to you, but your need for funds pulled me to you as well. We were inevitable."

"I told you we were. We're too irresistible." I kiss her long and slow, amazed at her resilience. She's been dealt a shit show today, yet here she lies next to me, seemingly relaxed and content. I'm starting to realise she wears a front. Her coping mechanisms are flight, mask or ignore and they're not healthy. She can't always flee and run away, she can't always hide behind a mask and she can't ignore the issues she needs to deal with.

Her upbringing was clearly not normal but when it's all you've ever known, you don't know any different. Looking after a sick parent through her teenage years is something I can't comprehend. Today was her ultimate wake up call. It started months ago when she took the first step to break out of her cage and find me. Fliss emerged in the time we spent together, she completely came out of her shell, her confidence soared. And now after piecing together why her parents were so hellbent on keeping her from the real world, she's truly awake, truly aware and truly able to move forward.

I'm just hoping I'll still fit with this new life she forges for herself.

The shift I feared, took hold regardless.

It was probably inevitable but still, it feels like a right hook to the gut.

Days have passed since Fliss found out the circumstances surrounding her birth. She's become increasingly distant with me and in turn I've tied myself up in knots worrying my fears are about to be recognised. Might as well face it head-on instead of this dancing around it.

Because let's face it, she doesn't know how to dance, her moves are jerky and uncoordinated. *They don't make sense.* I have to be the one to broach this and I'm going in with caution.

"What's wrong, Fliss? I know you've had a lot to deal with, that's an understatement, but you're shutting me out. You're distant with me and I don't know how to help. Talk to me." I plead

She looks up from the book she's reading "I'm sorry." She says and turns back to her fucking book.

Cold as ice.

It's all I ever hear. "I'm sorry." I mimic "That's all you say. Why does it feel like you're pulling away?" I inhale and hold, when I release it's on a whispered confession "It feels like I'm losing you."

She sighs as she adjusts on the armchair, curling her legs beneath herself and reluctantly angling my way "Ash I love you. I do. If I'm certain of anything right now it's that..."

"Why can I hear a but coming?"

Her gaze drops "Because I've realised something these last few days and haven't known how to break it to you."

I steel myself. This sounds a whole lot like a breakup speech. "How about you just say it?"

Her eyes whip up to meet mine, resolve aimed my way, "I need you to go back home for a while."

I thought I was ready for the direction this conversation was heading in, I was braced for it but still, hearing her say the words crush me. It *guts* me.

"What?!" It is the only word I'm able to get out. *Un fucking believable.*

"Ash, time became blurred for me. It was running out so quickly for my mum that I felt I had to speed up too. That's why I came to you. But I set out with better intentions than that for you. Now I need it to slow down again. I need to catch up to everything that's happened, all the ridiculous revelations. I need to know who Fliss is before the next shock comes along. And I need to do it alone. I need to truly figure out who I am, what I'm capable of without relying on others. *Without relying on you.* That scared me before. Being alone. I did everything in my power to avoid it. But I think it will be good for me now. In the end, it'll be good for us."

I shake my head, I'm still in a state of shock. I look over at her, and finally some emotion is shown. She's affected by this conversation as well, her watery eyes let me see that much. "I can't believe this." I tell her

"I'm just asking for some time. I don't want to lose you. But when you're here my thoughts are consumed by you. I can't breathe, Ash. That's the intensity of my feelings. I need to know they weren't just manufactured out of desperation and because I thought you were all I had. You need me to be your equal and right now I'm not up to scratch, but I want to be for you. I have work to do and you can't help."

"For God's sake, Fliss. There's nothing wrong with you. You don't need to work on yourself or any of the other shit you just said. You don't need to do anything other than be who you already are."

She shakes her head, disappointed that I don't get it, "But I don't know who I am. I pray it isn't who I've been because she was a liar, she used people. She wasn't a nice person. I've always been dictated to, directed, commanded and been expected to be a certain way. I've had staff that did everything for me. I've never had to stand on my own two feet. The minute I had to I wasn't ready for it, but now I am. I've matured so much and that's thanks to you, but I still have a long way to go."

"You don't honestly think I'm going to desert you while you're carrying my child do you? You need space that's fine, I'll sleep in a different room, but I can't fly back to Ireland."

"You have to, Ash. I don't want to send you away, God knows this will be easier with you by my side, but in the long run, it will be detrimental. I need to find my way without relying on someone else to give me the answers. How am I supposed to raise a child based on the example I was set? I won't even be able to cook for it because I never learnt how. I'm weeks away from turning 20 and I don't know how to use a washing machine or how to pay bills. I've never done something as simple and mundane as putting the rubbish out. What can I teach this child if I don't start educating myself on ordinary day to day tasks as opposed to languages I'll never use?"

I can see her mind is made up. I could push back. I want to. But I know whatever argument I put forward won't sway her and I'm not into begging. She wants me to leave, fine. I'll fucking leave. I won't stay where I'm not wanted. *Where I'm not needed.* I'll make this easy for her, but I won't be decent about it, "Dress it up however you like, Fliss. Convince yourself those are the reasons if you need to. It's about time I went home anyway." I rise from my chair, leave the room, slamming the door behind me as I do.

Felicity

Current mood – Thinking clearly... finally
Regret level – Visiting regrets r us regularly

Asking Ash to leave cut me to the quick. Sometimes the best decisions are the hardest and we have to do what we must to achieve what we need. There was no way around it. Because I had to learn to be alone. I had to learn to function without creating toxicity with those I claimed to love.

See, that's where I was wrong. I thought I loved him from afar, from the safety of my computer screen. But all I loved was the idea of him. The idea of us. I needed those interactions with someone unobtainable to dull the pain I was in, but it allowed me to create a fantasy so beyond reach when it did become in touching distance I thought I'd achieved all I ever wanted.

Make-believe can never hold up to the harsh light of day.

I didn't know what love was until I left him, until he found me again. My interpretation of love came from Disney films, princesses and heroes. It was a childish naivety. Real-life isn't at all like that. And like he once said to me – *love isn't the be-all and end-all.* It's a great starting point, but to make a relationship work there are so many other facets that need to go into it.

It's taken a while but I'm finally making moves, literally. I put my parents home up for sale. Gerry was happy to retire which made that particular decision easier. I purchased my first home from the sale, not to mention my inheritance was a large sum. My home is a modest 3 bedroom and is perfect for my needs. I still own Montgomery's manuscripts, I couldn't give it up but I've taken on a manager so I can focus on what I want to do in life. Figuring out my dream job is a head-scratcher, but I have time to get there. Finally, I can think about what I'd like to achieve, instead of what was expected of me. At the moment I'm clueless.

I've taken up cooking lessons. Once a week I go to class and learn a new recipe. Having my meals prepared for me is something I miss, but that's laziness, it's all part of my relearning or better still, unlearning what I'm used to. Not only that, but I've made friends, female friends. People who genuinely seem to like me and who I genuinely like in return. I've finally found my clique, women who will give me the 'talk' when I need it. They've been a breath of fresh air and much-needed company whilst I've allowed the real me to emerge and flourish.

I've wandered around the town centre, content to be by myself. I've shopped, for clothes other than onesies, I've developed a new kind of style, one that's both comfortable and I feel good in. My onesies will never be replaced completely but they have agreed to take a backseat... for the time being.

I've realised the only thing I can control is myself and how I treat others. That's it.

Living alone isn't as scary as I thought it would be. Not when you have peace inside yourself. Not when it's somewhere that's yours and doesn't hold bad memories. My new home is a safe haven. I love knowing it's mine, I love being there, decorating, making meals, taking care of myself. This part of my life hasn't been as daunting as I imagined.

The only thing missing is Ash.

I needed to know that although I loved him, I hadn't just latched on to him for the wrong reasons. Obviously, at the beginning I did, but would we have stayed together if I wasn't so afraid of being alone? If I wasn't so wrapped up in grief and then shock, if there had been someone else to lean on in his place, would I have relied on him as much? Would he have really stayed for anything other than support after my mother's passing and then our baby news?

Now I know I would have still chosen him. Because that's what relationships are about. I wish I'd found him after I'd figured my shit out, once I'd matured and experienced being single, confident, capable Fliss. But if I'd waited for that, fate probably would have led me down another route, far away from him and we'd never have even met. The forks in the road are there to test us. I wonder sometimes if the higher powers watch as we take the wrong path and shake their heads at our missed opportunities. Do they sit around watching us living, taking wagers on which way we'll go, right or wrong, misery or happiness, death or living. Do they celebrate when we get it right? I truly believe I had to go through all those devastating things, things that could have destroyed me so I could figure out who I truly am. And guess what? I like me, flaws and all. I've been empowered from learning to like my own company. It's true that we need to love ourselves before someone else can, otherwise we'll always wonder what they see, doubt our worth and drive them away because of it.

Sending him away stung, it nearly crippled me and sent me back to the dark hole I crawled out of before I met him. The knowledge that this time I was doing it on purpose made it all the more cruel.

As much as I used to rely on fate and still believe in it to a degree. I also know I have the power to go after what I want. There isn't always something whispering in my ear, suggesting the choices I make. I relied on looking for signs everywhere that I was doing the right thing and more often than not I wasn't. Now, I trust myself. Wanting something doesn't mean we're entitled to it. Sometimes we have to work hard to prove we deserve it. And that's what I've done. I've worked so hard on myself and now I can prove to Ash that I'm deserving of his love, because before, I always had a question mark over it. I didn't deserve him. I lied and tricked and used him.

He's about to find out how much he means to me in the only way I can communicate it to him.

Ashton

The last few months have been testing to say the least. Having to break the news to my parents and friends that I got Fliss pregnant but we're no longer together was a fun conversation. I didn't think it was possible for my dad to be anymore disappointed in me than he already was but the way he exploded said otherwise. My mother cried, both from happiness at knowing she was having a grandchild to sadness that she'd rarely see the baby. Trina hugged me, then punched me in my arm for leaving without a word. And the guys helped me to get drunk.

Fliss is about 6 months now. We stay in touch by phone and Facebook, we're awkwardly polite as she fills me in on how the pregnancy progresses, when the scans are, results of blood tests and all the appointments I miss out on attending. She's stolen this from me and day by day resentment seeps in. We've agreed I should go back to London closer to her due date so I can be there for the birth, but I feel alienated, as though this is happening to someone else. I want to be more included. I want to have a proper family, where my child grows up with both parents and because I still love her. The void between us has grown, as I knew it would. Long-distance relationships are hard work, especially when one half doesn't want it. I didn't choose this for us. I've had no say and have still been expected to be cool with the outcome. We still have an undeniable connection, but it's holding on by a thread. It's being tested yet hasn't broken. I have no choice but to love her from a distance.

I respect why she asked me to leave. Actually, that's horseshit. I despised her at first. I couldn't speak to her for the first week after I arrived home. But as the months have gone on I've come to understand... ish. It was a brave choice. It doesn't mean I liked it. But isn't the saying 'If you love something, let it go?' I wasn't going to stay where I wasn't wanted. She's had a rollercoaster of a year, needing time to unravel that is a fair expectation.

But I still don't fucking like it.

And so like most days, I write and then sit with my phone in my hand willing it to ring before I can dial. Neither happens, I have to take any scraps she can offer up, when she can fit me in. Sounds a lot like bitterness, right? Because it is. I've already sensed the change in her and I'm worried one day soon she'll tell me she's done, she's found herself and realised I no longer factor in her future.

I place the defective phone on my coffee table, walk to the kitchen and grab a drink from the fridge. Our rules list is still pinned up. The 'no being annoying' rule Fliss demanded glares at me every time, because she's the one being annoying and frustrating.

The door knocks and I walk towards it, pulling it open to see another delivery of bills.

And a package.

I sign for the box, close the door awkwardly as it's so heavy and sit back down wondering what I might have ordered.

I rip it open to find books, a shit ton of books. When I pull one out, I take in the front cover, the image is a crisp white cover with a picture of Fliss and I, taken on my phone one morning when we were in bed. She's nuzzling her face against me. At the time, I'm not even sure she knew I'd captured us, I sent it to her after I'd left and told her it was my favourite picture, caught in a natural moment. Neither of us posing or smiling, we weren't looking at the camera because we only had eyes for each other. Around the image is a reddish hue, almost like clouds of smoke, concealing everything except our faces. *Concealing the lies.* The title reads **Sweet Deceit** and both our names are printed as authors – mine first and hers underneath.

I slouch back. I can't believe she finished our story. I can't believe it's published and I'm holding a paperback copy in my hand. I turn it over and read the blurb:

How far would you go to escape circumstances out of your control?

Impulsiveness isn't something Fliss Montgomery is familiar with. Until a moment of clarity causes her to make a split- second decision, and the answer becomes as easy as breathing.

Fly across the world on nothing more than a whim.

Her destination – Ashton Blake, the oblivious object of her affection and the stranger she talks to every day from the anonymity of a computer screen.

Only he has no idea she's coming and when she arrives at his doorstep, he mistakes her for a potential flat mate. Instead of correcting him, she moves in.

Fliss is about to realise no matter how far you run, happiness can't be built on a cocktail of fantasy and lies.

And deceit doesn't really taste all that sweet.

Precise and to the point. If I'd had any input I probably would have droned on for far too long. I open the pages and see my dedication to her is still there, but she's also included one to me:

"If you find someone who knows all your mistakes, accepts them,

forgives you for them and loves you in spite of them, never let them go."

This first book off the pile has a yellow sticky note underneath the quote that reads *I found that someone and let him go. How dumb am I? I've taken more than I've given. I've forced patience on you while you let me find the best version of myself. You didn't try to change me but let me realise I didn't have to change, I just needed to grow. I just needed you.*

I digest those words slowly. It's an apology of sorts and though I'm sick and tired of her explaining her feelings via writing my heart picks up a pace at the hope contained within them. Fliss has always been more open through writing, through email interactions, through any means other than face to face.

I get comfortable. I know what I wrote, from the time she turned up on my doorstep and I believed she was only here to view the apartment, right up until our shock baby news. But reading what her motives were and how she felt for that time period is an insight I can't wait to get lost in. As always, understanding her is my number one priority. She might drip feed information to me but at least I get it.

And for the rest of the day that's exactly what I do. I'm engrossed in reading a love story about my life and how a onesie wearing woman came along and changed it for the better.

Epilogue

Putting your life out there for complete strangers to have an opinion on can go one or two ways.

Firstly it can be enjoyed, make you a bestseller and create a huge fan following. Because reading a true story about two regular people makes others believe this kind of life is accessible. If we found our soul mate through the means we did, then they can too. Our story was relatable, crazy maybe and more suited to a work of fiction, but still...

Our honesty, our struggles and our love, written from both our points of view was a hit.

But here comes the secondly, with that comes the negativity, the judgement and the backlash. The downright tearing down of Fliss' character because she made mistakes, she made plenty, but she held her hands up, she admitted to them and then included them in this book of our life. Social media helps in this business, to keep you relevant, to have your work seen, to interact with readers but it also opens up a can of worms. Keyboard warriors use it as a place to insult, to tear you down. To send private messages and directly tell you their thoughts on everything they deem you did wrong. It's fine to disagree with our story. It's not fine to bully because of a differing opinion.

How often do you make mistakes? I'm guessing regularly because as humans it's human nature to do so. No one is perfect. It's strange to me that complete strangers think they have any sort of right to judge us, to have an opinion on our relationship but this is the attention we invited in when we released this story. It's part and parcel of now being well known, but the invasive questions Fliss gets asked about her parents and Milly is shocking. Thank God the only real names we used in this were our own, because of the selling a child part, that caused an uproar.

If we've brought out such strong emotions in readers, though then I guess it was written well.

To be honest I don't much care either way anymore because after I read it, I did a Fliss. Dropped everything, flew to her on a whim and moved in. I haven't left since and nothing could ever make me again. A few weeks ago our baby girl was born and life as a dad is utter bliss or utter Fliss as I like to say. Whatever went before, from the day she was born I knew I was the luckiest guy alive, my two beautiful girls are thriving, happy and healthy.

Freya's birth even softened my father. Grey should now be called rainbow or some other stupid play on how happy he is. I had no idea he was such a softy, but then my girl brought me to my knees. They're even planning on moving over as they can't bear the distance apart.

Me, I'm still writing. I'm sought after now and God did it feel good to shove that in my fathers face. To prove him wrong. He took it well, begrudgingly but he even said he was proud of me. Blow me over with a fucking feather. I still leave her shower smiley's whenever I can, sometimes we simply shower together and I make her more than smile in there. She still opens packets of sweets before me and bins the nasty green ones. It's definitely the little things in life that have the biggest meaning.

And Fliss...

Would you believe out of everything she could do she decided her talents lay in designing? Not any old designing though, no, Fliss designed a range of baby animal onesies – seriously, you should see the octopus design. She used our precious baby as a model for the first photoshoot, if I thought her cow onesie with the four dicks was bad, well this grey thing had eight limbs. I couldn't stay and watch because I was starting to choke on my laughter. If you think that's funny, imagine me, the poor guy who had to walk around with his fiancé dressed as a caterpillar while holding our bundle of cuteness who was in a butterfly onesie, widespread wings and all. It was kinda cute I guess, I know what she was going for, but fuck me. People must have looked at us and thought we were on day release from a loony house or something. Luckily she only did that in public the once to teach me a lesson. And it's one of the greatest things about her. She doesn't care what others think of her clothing choices. It doesn't embarrass her and to be that free must be a glorious feeling. I know I couldn't do it. Her own onesies don't make as much of an appearance any more which I must admit, I miss. Every now and then she likes to surprise me with a ludicrous design she's found which she wears around the house. She does it completely on purpose, she knows my absolute weakness where they're concerned are the ones with tails and hoods and I'm betting it won't be long before she moves into designing adult ones for nothing more than to humiliate me.

Fliss never did meet with Millie. And for that I'm grateful. I don't know what she wanted to gain from it, but I worried if she was expecting some kind of relationship to form she'd be disappointed. She toyed with the idea so many times but ultimately decided the woman was nothing to her, she already had her answers and once our baby was born she really couldn't understand why anyone would sell their child. Maybe someday in the faraway future, she'll revisit her decision and if she does I'll stand by her. But for now, we're focusing on being happy, on being parents and soaking up this new experience for both of us.

So life worked out the way we wanted. Fliss always tells me she knew if we could just meet, even for the briefest of moments our relationship would be cemented. She didn't expect there to be so many bumps in the road, but anything worth having isn't always going to be easy.

It was a chaotic way to get here. There were times I thought we'd be forever severed. She kept me on my toes, but ultimately, if Fliss hadn't committed that Sweet Deceit I'd never know how perfect my life could be.

The End

Bonus chapter
(Excerpt from Sweet Deceit)
The first time we met

Ash

I've been cleaning this apartment like a maniac. Making a good impression on this viewing is essential. I'm generally a clean and tidy guy anyway but making this extra effort might just cinch it for me.

This viewing has to work out.

I don't know how Cammy has been finding out about the others but if this bad luck streak continues because she gets a whiff of this one and fucks it up again, I might have to move home.

And that is something to be avoided at all costs.

I take one last look around just to check all is satisfactory and curse as my phone rings. If this is the interested party ringing to cancel, I'm screwed.

Jake's name flashes on the screen, "Hey." I answer

"Trina's done it again. You better get over here."

"On my way," I reply, no questions asked.

Trina is one of my best mates, has been since we were kids, but she has her own demons to battle, every now and then she fails miserably and we all have to rally to be by her side. She needs me and that is possibly the only thing that could make me cancel this viewing.

"Fuck!" I shout, slamming my hand on the breakfast bar. "Why does she do this?" I mutter to myself. Her timing sucks but I know she doesn't have any control, she doesn't purposely choose when these episodes will occur.

I make my way to the door and just as I reach it, it knocks. I consult my watch, noticing the woman is early. I can't cancel now, but I can make this quick.

I pull the door open, a little too forcefully in my impatience to get going. The woman stood before me has her head downcast, staring at her shoes. Long blonde hair is all I can see, she has mounds of it, as though she's never had a haircut her whole life, it easily goes past her arse.

She suddenly flicks her head my way and our eyes connect. Hers are an ocean blue filled with sadness, she looks so timid, awkward as she stands before me, wringing her hands and swaying on the spot as if her modest heels are too much for her to handle.

A small smile plays over her lips as she drinks me in. She's cute. But I don't have time to put on a charm offensive.

"You just going to stand there, or are you coming in?" *Nice one, Ash, real welcoming.*

She walks past me like Bambi, tottering in those shoes, as I close the door and take her in. Oh yeah, that hair is Rapunzel length long. I bet it's great to pull on in the bedroom.

I clear my throat before thoughts like that can lead down a dangerous path, walking past her I say. "I'm sorry but I've managed to double book myself, this will have to be a quick tour." I stride ahead of her, desperate to get this over with.

"Living room." I tell her before moving on to the next room "Bathroom."

I stop outside the spare room "This is the spare room." I continue, opening the door and moving aside so she can look in. She takes a quick peek before turning to face me.

"So, what do you think?" I ask, turning and quickly glancing at my watch.

"Umm, uh... your home is lovely." She stutters. She looks like she wants to say more, but the way she stares at me is kind of disconcerting, if I didn't know better I'd say she was swimming with recognition. I realise she sounds completely different to the woman I spoke to on the phone.

My brows rise "Not from around here?"

"What gave me away?"

"The accent for one. Look, I'm late for something so do you want the room or not?" I hate myself for being this tactless and emotionless, but my worry for Trina has only intensified and I just want to leave. Finding a roommate doesn't now hold the same urgency it did 20 minutes ago.

"Huh?" she asks

"You're here for the spare room, right?" I question as my brow raises. For a split second, I contemplate this could be a new trick of Cammy's.

"Yeah, right." She agrees quickly.

"So? Are you my new roommate or not?" I can barely hide the desperation in my voice. I silently compel her to agree.

"Me?" She blurts as though such a thing is absolutely absurd. *Then why are you here? Wasting my damn time!*

I squint at her and after what feels like an age she says "Yes, I'll take it."

I can't help but smile. This woman, without even knowing it has just solved all of my problems. I could hug her for that alone. But this isn't a done deal yet. I need to lock her in so she can't back out and put me back to square one.

"Good. So Uh if you have the first months rent, we're good to go." I run through some on the details we spoke about over the phone and running through some quick ground rules. I direct her over to my kitchen island and show her the pre prepared paperwork I had drafted.

"Right, so the paperwork is here, and this is the spare key. I've signed already so feel free to peruse it and if happy it's a done deal. I know this is unorthodox and I'm really sorry to dump you like this, but I really do have to go. I'll be back later so feel free to make yourself at home, acclimatise, whatever and if you need to move your things in while I'm gone, please do. We can catch up later, roomie?" As I talk, she avoids all eye contact, looking through the contract in front of her instead.

I frown when she hands over a stack of cash, but convince myself she's probably just drawn it out in preparation of her acceptance.

"Okay." She agrees reluctantly and I wish I didn't have to leave like this. I have time though to show her my first impression may have been lacklustre but living with me will be fun. I nod at her agreement, smile her way and leave. Leaning against the door once I'm in the hall. What the fuck did I just do?

ACKNOWLEDGMENTS

A huge thank you has to go to Sarah Louise Brown, who has helped endlessly with this book. The tagline came about from brainstorming with her, she was one of the first to read the draft chapters and then she beta read for me as well. You. Are. A. Gem.

Massive thank you also to my other beta's – Yvonne Eason, Donna Matthewman, and Linda Humphries – your input was invaluable.

Kerry Humphreys – This book would likely still not be finished if you hadn't sprinted with me for the last stretch and held me accountable. You are always there with ready advice and I'm so thankful for you. The teasers you designed are gorgeous and I'm so lucky to have you as a friend. Love you muchly!

Emma Louise Norton James and Vicky Shellard – There are lots of pieces in this story that came from spending time with you guys. Thanks for being some of the driving inspiration behind it.

Stella Gray – Although the first half of this was light and a little comedic, I always knew the illness of Fliss' mother would be the driving factor for her leaving. I researched Alzheimers and dementia because I wanted to convey the truth of these awful illnesses, but having never been affected by it I knew I needed the input of someone who had. Thank you so much Stella for reading the chapters I sent to you and for your openness and honesty.

Amanda Walker – For the amazing book cover. I loved it the moment I saw it. Thank you!

Rebecca Milhoan – For editing and making the words I wrote readable. You're a star and I can't thank you enough for jumping on board and helping with this.

And to you, the readers. You make this possible. Thank you for taking a chance on an indie author. I hope you enjoyed reading Ash and Fliss' story.

Share your thoughts

If you enjoyed reading this novel, please consider leaving a review on Amazon and Goodreads. Reviews help indie authors immensely by spreading the word. I read each and every review myself. I love to connect with my readers so feel free to drop me a line.

Printed in Great Britain
by Amazon

87142688R00122